The Summer 10

E. Reimer

Saguaro Books, LLC
SB
Arizona

Saguaro Books, LLC
16845 E. Avenue of the Fountains, Ste. 325
Fountain Hills, AZ 85268
www.saguarobooks.com

ISBN: 978-1-0881-9636-6
Library of Congress Cataloging Number
LCCN: 2022944670
Printed in the United States of America
First Edition

Dedication

Dedicated to my Father: thank you for all the gifts

To my family: you created an environment where imagination and creativity could bloom in my mind. You planted instrumental seeds of faith in my soul, which continue to produce fruit. You have pushed me, believed in me and let me rest in unending security. You are victorious warriors in a blind world.

To Dorothy, Isaac, Lena, Abram and Bert: thank you for your legacies

1

The wind rustled the oak leaves as Finley climbed into his tree house. He lowered a basket to Leah, who placed an unlit lantern inside, along with a box of cookies, a thermos of cocoa and two mugs.

"OK," she whispered and signalled for him to lift the bundle. She followed closely behind.

The two friends stifled their laughter as they settled themselves in the middle of the house. Pillows and blankets made the floor cozy and the moon provided enough light to cast mystical shadows along the walls.

"Here." Finley shone his flashlight onto the lantern so Leah could find the switch.

"Thanks." She carefully hung it on a hook in the center of the roof.

He poured out the cocoa and gave Leah a mug.

"OK, can you finally tell me what's going on?" she asked, "and why did we have to sneak out tonight?"

He grinned mischievously. "I think of it as preparing for our summer."

Leah bit into a cookie and smirked. "Oh? What are we gonna do, rob a bank?"

He rolled his eyes. "Of course not."

"Well then what is it, Finn? You've been driving me crazy since you passed me that note at lunch to meet you here. What's up?"

Finley held out his hand. "First, you have to pinkie promise you won't tell anyone about my plan. You can back out of it if you want but just don't tell anyone. OK?"

"Yeah, whatever." Leah quickly linked her pinkie with his. "Now, what is it?"

The lantern made it look as though his eyes were twinkling. "This is the last summer before high school."

"Duh."

"Which means next year my dad will make me get a summer job."

"He said that?"

"Yeah. For the past two years now he's been saying I have to get a summer job when I'm in high school." He sipped his cocoa. "Which means this is our last chance to hang out all summer."

Leah wiped cookie crumbs from her hands. "So, what do you want to do?"

"Remember how we always wanted to buy a whole pail of ice cream and eat it in one day?"

She laughed. "Oh yeah. We never had enough cash to do that."

"Or sneak out at night and go to the beach when no one is there—"

"To hunt crabs," Leah interrupted, "and we've never gone to the theater and snuck into an R-rated movie."

"Exactly." Finley pulled out a small notebook and pencil from his back pocket. "I think we should make a list of stuff we've wanted to do since we were kids. We'll do everything on it and have the best summer of our lives."

Leah laughed. "Wow, Finn, I'm surprised. I'm usually the one to plan things."

"What are you talking about? I plan things."

"You think about the stuff we need," she agreed, "but I'm the one who always says we need to research stuff before we start anything. Remember our Alka Seltzer rocket for the science fair?"

Finley shrugged. "It worked…"

"And our test run exploded in your face because you didn't research everything first; the amount of Alka Seltzer to use, how much water, the temperature it needed to be…"

"OK, OK, moving on. The summer list, are you in or out?"

She laughed again. "I'm in. Where do we start?"

"You still have your bike from last year, right?"

She nodded. "Yeah. It's a little small now but I can ride it."

"Great. That takes care of transportation. Now for supplies… We'll need to buy some stuff to actually do the things on our list. You know, ice cream or movie tickets for example. I have some birthday money we can use."

Rain began to drizzle outside and Leah drew a blanket up to her shoulders. "I've got about thirty bucks I can add to that."

"Cool." He looked up at her and smiled. "So, what do you want to add to the list?"

She mulled the question over for a few moments then said, "I want to take a dance class."

"What?" Finley frowned. "That sounds so boring."

"Just one class," she insisted. "Come on, we're going into high school. That means there'll be school dances. I don't want to be that one boring girl in the corner watching everyone else dance."

"Blech." Finley grabbed his stomach and pretended to throw up.

Leah crossed her arms. "Whatever. Got any better ideas?"

"I want to build something with my own hands, with no help from my parents."

"Since when have you wanted to do that?"

"I dunno." Finley tapped his pencil on his knee. "Maybe when my Dad built this tree house?"

She agreed. "It's an awesome hangout place."

"I know, right? And I wanna give it a try."

"Fine," Leah relented. "What do you want to build?"

Finley beamed. "I'm thinking a throne."

"What?" Leah's mouth gaped open. "If I'm helping you build a throne, I definitely want you to write 'take a dance class' on the list."

He sighed. "All right, I'll add it."

The rest of the list formed quickly, with both parties agreeing to each item. It had been years in the making.

Leah and Finn's List for an Awesome Summer

1. Eat a whole gallon of ice cream (each)
2. Build a throne
3. Take a dance class
4. Hunt crabs at night, at the beach
5. Sneak into an R rated movie at the theater
6. Drive a car
7. Discover a new world
8. Stay awake for 24 hours straight
9. Find buried treasure
10. Attempt a world record

We hereby commit to having the best summer ever by completing every item on this list to our best ability,

Leah Harris

Finley Davidson

Thursday, June 24, 1993

2

"Hey, Finn." Leah got up from the floor as he reached his locker. "How do you think you did?"

Finley shrugged. "I think I did all right. The multiple choice questions were fine but I wasn't sure what to write for my essay."

A boy with curly red hair walked out of the classroom. "Tough exam," he said, as he passed them. "Glad it's over and I can forget all that junk we had to study. Make room for more important stuff, you know?"

Leah murmured to Finley, "How to cheat in video games, for instance?"

The red-haired boy overheard her and beamed. "Exactly."

"What are you gonna do this summer, Lewis?" Finley asked.

Lewis opened his locker and took out all his binders. "My stepdad wants to take me camping." He carried his school notes and old papers in a messy pile then dumped them into the nearest recycling bin. "But we won't get to if my mom has anything to say about it. She hates the idea of me even getting a splinter. She's like, 'Ew. Get it out. Sanitize that. Don't get infected. Take off your bandage. No, get away. Don't chase me with that thing.'" Lewis laughed.

Leah raised an eyebrow. "You chased your mom with a bandage?"

Lewis's face turned scarlet from laughing so hard. "Just once. I think I traumatized her, though. Since then, she's been even more of a germophobe." He slammed his empty locker shut and hooked a backpack strap over his shoulder. "Anyway, I don't wanna spend another second here. I've had too many nightmares about this place. Catch you guys later."

"Later." Finley nodded.

"See you around." Leah smiled.

"I heard Joy's having a party tonight." Finley turned to her. "Everyone's going to bring their schoolwork and burn it in a huge bonfire at her place."

"Yeah, she invited me to come. She said I could stay the night at her place, too."

"Oh?" Finley looked disappointed for a moment but his face cleared quickly. Leah only had a few good friends so when she had plans, he didn't know about he was always caught off guard.

"We should go," Leah said, as they cleaned out their own lockers. "It'll be fun."

He nodded. "Yeah, all right."

"I know I sound uncool but…shouldn't we recycle our stuff, too?"

Finley's brow furrowed. "Then what'll we burn?"

Leah shrugged. "Hot dogs and marshmallows?"

He patted her arm. "You're right. You sound super uncool."

Leah walked over to Finley's house around 6 o'clock. His dad answered the doorbell.

"Good evening, Leah." He smiled. "How are you today?"

"Great, Mr. Davidson." She smiled back. "Grade eight is officially over and I've got the whole summer ahead of me."

He looked at the backpack, sleeping bag and bag of marshmallows she was holding. "Oh, do you have extra plans tonight?"

"Yeah, I'm staying at Joy's after the party. I won't need a ride home."

"Are you parents picking you up later?"

"Yep. Dad's getting a haircut tomorrow so he'll pick me up before his appointment."

Finley appeared behind his father. "Ready to go?"

They all got into the car, Finley and Leah in the backseat.

"I suppose you both will be driving soon," Mr. Davidson said, as he glanced at them from his rear-view mirror.

Leah looked at the dashboard and gearshift. "I'm so excited." She squealed. "My mom wants to teach me how to drive a stick shift first. She said it'll be easier to drive any car after that."

Mr. Davidson paused at a stop sign and checked the road before proceeding. "Interesting idea. We prefer automatic vehicles ourselves. I expect this car will be the first one you drive, Finley. Do you remember where your hands should be positioned on the wheel?"

"Ten and two o'clock," he replied confidently.

"And the gearshift?" his dad continued. "What letter should it be in when you're going somewhere?"

"D for drive," Finley answered. "Unless you're going backwards, of course. Then it should be R for reverse."

His dad chuckled. "Can't trick you, even if I try."

"Nope," Finley said and popped one of Leah's marshmallows into his mouth. "I've heard them all by now."

Leah raised an eyebrow in his direction. "You're not going to toast it first?"

He grinned and offered her one. She refused.

Mr. Davidson continued, "I've still got a few tricks saved for when you're older."

With a full mouth, Finley asked, "What are they?"

His dad laughed. "I don't want to spoil the surprise."

They laughed in a similar manner and Leah looked out the window. She was lost in her own thoughts, as they passed by the familiar neighborhoods and entered a landscape of open fields and far horizons. *I always like seeing the countryside around here. Where people haven't claimed the earth and trained it to do whatever they want. A tree can grow as tall and aged as it desires. Unharnessed weeds can crawl wherever they like and flowers can stretch their petals to embrace the sun's rays.*

"What about you, Leah?" Mr. Davidson suddenly broke through her thoughts.

Her gaze refocused onto his face in the rear-view mirror. "What was that?"

"What are you looking forward to about high school?"

"Oh, um…" she pondered. "I've heard the cafeteria food is better."

Finley chuckled. "No, he means what elective classes are you gonna take?"

"Oh." She cleared her throat. "Well, I want to take art for sure and psychology."

"That's an interesting combination," Mr. Davidson commented.

"I'm thinking of becoming an art therapist," she replied. "But I don't know for sure. Architecture's also interesting but I don't know if I'd enjoy the engineering part of it. The next gravel road is the one you need to take."

They turned onto it and headed east. Mr. Davidson continued, "There's lots of time to figure out what you want to do when you're older. You may as well take advantage of all your options now and try a little of everything."

Finley asked, "When did you know you wanted to be a pharmacist, Dad?"

"Oh," he mulled, "I suppose it was about the time when you were born. I realized I couldn't goof around anymore. Suddenly, there were more bills and one less paycheck in our household."

Finley was quiet and his whole body sagged deeper into the backseat. He resembled a guilty puppy as he stared out the window. His father noticed the mood shift and added quietly, "But I wouldn't change anything if I had to do it over again."

"This is the place, Mr. Davidson." Leah pointed to their left.

They pulled onto a farmyard driveway. Maple trees lined both sides, as though escorting them toward the house. Leah had been at the farm for a Christmas party last year and loved seeing the fresh snow on their branches but it gave them a sleepy feeling. Their brilliant green leaves now inspired energy and excitement, as though they were also invited to the party.

"I haven't been here in forever," Finley mentioned.

She looked at him. "When's the last time?"

"For a birthday party. I think she turned seven that year…You know, the one where Lewis got sick and threw up on the kitchen floor while we sang Happy Birthday?"

Leah laughed. "Oh, I totally forgot about that. So gross."

He chuckled. "Hope we don't have a repeat performance tonight."

"I hope you're not hinting about him getting drunk." Mr. Davidson parked the car and looked back at them.

"Nah, that won't happen," Leah reassured him. "Besides, Joy's parents are here. If anyone even tried sneaking in alcohol, they'd be banned for life. It's not worth the risk of missing out on the fun."

He nodded. "All right then. Leah, make sure you've got all your stuff; Finley, you'll call me when you're ready to be picked up?"

"Yep."

"OK, I'll see you later. Have fun, you two."

Leah and Finley spilled out of the car and strolled over to the backyard where they could hear music and laughter. A large pile of wood stood in a cleared-off area with lawn chairs set up around it. Several kids were standing around, chatting with drinks in their hands. Joy saw them approach and met them halfway.

"Hey guys." She beamed her typical hundred-watt smile at them, the kind movie stars dreamed of having.

"Hey," Leah and Finley replied in unison.

"Thanks for coming. I see you're all ready for our sleepover." She winked at Leah. "We're totally pulling an all-nighter."

Leah smiled. "So, we're watching movies and raiding the kitchen in the middle of the night?"

Joy nodded. "You know it. What did we end up eating last time…was it mac and cheese with Oreos?"

Leah laughed. "It was mac and cheese with M&Ms. I can't believe we actually ate it."

"Hey, it was, like, two in the morning and we were starving."

Finley held up the bag of marshmallows. "Here, this'll help."

Joy took the bag from him. "Thanks. My parents bought, like, five bags already but you can never have enough marshmallows. You guys want a drink or something to eat?"

"Yeah," Finley said.

Leah asked, "Can I put my stuff in your house first?"

"Sure thing, I'll help." She grabbed Leah's sleeping bag then turned to Finley and pointed in the direction of the drinks. "Cups and stuff are on the table over there."

The girls went in the house as Finley walked over. He scanned the drinks before choosing a can of orange soda.

His buddy Bryce suddenly appeared at his side and slapped him on the back. "Hey, Finn, I didn't know you were showing up tonight."

"Oh, hey, Bryce. Yeah, it was kind of a last-minute decision. I just assumed you'd be here, otherwise I would've told you earlier."

"Dude, can you believe we're done? We're going to high school in the fall, I'm totally buggin'."

Finley laughed. "Yeah, it's weird. After writing today's exam, I bounced outta there as fast as I could."

Bryce frowned. "Bounced?"

Finley nodded. "Yeah. You know, it means to leave…"

"Oh, yeah. Sure." Bryce pretended to have understood all along. "Anyway, I've been saving all my loose change for months, just to spend it at the arcade."

"You're going tomorrow?"

Bryce grinned. "Yeah, wanna come?"

"Sorry dude, I don't think I'll have a ride. My mom's doing the grocery shopping tomorrow and Dad said something about changing the oil in our car."

"I keep forgetting you don't live in the middle of the city where all the action is."

"I've always lived in the suburbs, Bryce."

"Yeah." Bryce shrugged. "I guess since my family moved a couple years ago, I assume everyone lives within walking distance of the arcade, movie theater and restaurants."

"Some other time," Finley said. "I definitely want to challenge you at Frogger this summer. It's about time I slash your high score to pieces."

"Nah, I don't play much Frogger anymore. All that frog does is hop across a street? Nah. That's boring. Mario Bros. That's where it's at."

"All right, you're on."

They tapped their cans together in agreement.

Finn asked, "So, what else are you up to this summer?"

"Not much, just hanging out," Bryce replied. "Oh, my cousin Rob is coming over for a couple weeks in August. We'll probably go to the water park every day and dominate the water slides. It's finally our year to take the park over from the little kids, ha."

"Is he the one that—"

"A couple years ago got his swimming trunks caught on the small diving board and they split in half as he fell into the pool? Yep, that's the one."

Finley laughed. "From what I heard, they ripped and only showed a little of his butt."

"Whatever. It was still wicked embarrassing."

Finley asked, "And you already convinced him to go back there?"

Bryce shrugged. "Not yet but I will."

Leah and Joy ran over to the bonfire area. Joy's mom followed behind with matches and newspaper.

"Guys, we're ready to start the fire," Joy announced.

There were about fifty kids on the yard and the setting sun was just starting to color the sky with hues of red, yellow and purple. Joy's mom started the blaze. Within minutes, kids whooped and hollered as it grew and overtook the whole bundle of wood. Some threw their old schoolwork in while others attempted to get near enough to roast hot dogs and marshmallows. Lewis tried poking a hole through a bunch of chips and roasting them but they kept falling into the fire. Around 11 o'clock, things started to settle down and the number of kids dwindled as parents picked them up.

"Leah." Finley came up to her. "I got a great idea for when we try staying awake for twenty-four hours."

The right side of her face glowed fire-orange as she turned to him. "What?"

"We should read ghost stories. They'll keep us awake the whole night."

"Ooh, I like it."

"What do you like?" Joy approached and offered them each a hot dog.

"We've got a few plans for the summer." Leah shook her head to reject the snack but Finley took one. "We're just working on a few details–"

Joy's dad called over from the back door of the house, "Joy, can you find Bryce? His brother is here to pick him up."

"Sure, Dad," she replied and went to search for him.

"I should be going too," Finley said. "Dad won't want to stay up too late because of me."

"I guess it's getting late." Leah nodded.

"Hey, um…are you gonna tell people about our plans for the summer?" Finley asked.

Leah shrugged. "I dunno. Why? You don't want me to?"

Finley repeated the shrug.

She frowned. "Well, are you gonna tell people?"

"I mean…if someone asks me what I'm doing…I might just say I'm busy."

"Why?"

"I dunno. I mean, we're not kids anymore but we're doing stuff we wanted to do as kids."

"Oh yeah. I hadn't thought of that."

Finley shook his head. "And I don't think our other friends will understand."

"They'll think it's stupid," Leah added, "and probably make fun of us."

"Exactly."

She nodded. "You're right. We should keep it a secret."

"It'll be just between us." He winked.

"Booyah." Lewis ran around the fire, hollering in victory.

"I think he finally toasted a chip," Finley remarked as they watched him.

Lewis stopped running and gingerly tasted the chip. After nothing happened, he put the rest in his mouth and crunched. His shoulders slumped as he walked past them toward the house. They heard him mutter to himself, "It…it doesn't taste any different. All that work, and nothing."

3

"I have a couple VHS tapes of *Saved by the Bell*," Joy announced to all the girls who were staying overnight. By midnight all the other kids had left, the fire was drowned out by the water hose and the remaining four girls were in their pj's, nestled among pillows, blankets and bowls of popcorn on the floor of Joy's basement.

"I love Slater," gushed Dawn.

"Uh-uh." Joy wagged a finger. "Zack-attack all the way."

"Have you seen Slater's dimples?" Dawn giggled. "I could go swimming in them. He's a total jock and his muscles prove it."

Leah stuck out her tongue. "Ewww, no. He's way too much of a ladies man. And what's with calling Jessie 'Mama' all the time?"

"Zack is just as much of a ladies man," Dawn retorted.

"But he can also stop time," Joy pointed out. "Imagine all the things you could do with that power."

"No, he can't," Leah argued. "That's just so we can hear his thoughts. He isn't actually stopping time."

Joy replied smugly, "Oh yeah? Then how does he dodge Slater's punch in that one episode?"

"Zack does some terrible stuff though," Dawn replied. "He takes advantage of others and then talks himself out of trouble before they get too angry. He's way meaner than Slater."

Leah shrugged. "He makes up for it. He always apologizes and changes."

"What do you think, Lauren?" Joy asked.

Lauren smiled shyly. "They're both nice…but Slater's my favorite."

"Then it's a tie." Joy declared and pressed play on the VHS player. "We can all agree that Screech is a skinny, nerdy goofball, right?"

All the girls agreed as they passed the popcorn around. They finished two episodes before they ran out of snacks.

"Out of all the guys in our class, who's the Slater?" Dawn asked with a gleam in her eye.

"Eww." Joy squealed. "None of them are muscular enough."

"James has the dimples though," Leah said.

"Yeah, he's cute," Dawn giggled.

"Dawn has a crush on James," Joy sang.

"Well, you like Reid," Dawn retorted.

Joy's face burned red. "That was a secret."

The group suddenly turned quiet. All eyes were on Joy and Dawn, waiting to see if a fight would start.

Leah broke the tension. "OK, confession time. We'll all swear to secrecy and say who we have a crush on. Then everything's fair." She looked at Joy to confirm peace was restored to the group.

"Sounds good to me," Joy replied. "You all know mine now. Who's yours, Dawn?"

Dawn lifted her chin proudly. "You were right. It's James. Bryce is kinda cute too but he brags about himself way too much."

Leah smiled. "Grant is pretty nice. And he's got amazing eyes."

"I like his style," Joy added. "I thought you'd say Finley though."

Leah felt the blood leave her face. "Finn? As if. We're just friends."

"Really?" Dawn prodded, "I thought you were dating."

"So did I," Joy said.

"Who told you that?" Leah asked.

"No one," said Joy, "but you guys hang out a lot."

"And you've known each other since you were little," Dawn said.

Leah tried to quickly put an end to the rumors. "Um, no offense but eww. It would be as if I was dating one of my cousins."

Dawn shrugged. "Well, I think he's kinda cute."

Leah's pulse slowed as the girls accepted her answer. She hadn't realized people thought she was dating Finley. They'd never talked about the subject with each other but as far as she knew, he was just as interested in dating her as she was him. Which was zero. They were buddies, nothing more. Just the thought of kissing his cheek made her queasy.

"Lauren, you're the last one," Dawn said.

Lauren blushed and looked at the floor. "I don't know," she mumbled.

"Uh-uh, not fair." Joy shook her head. "We all said ours. Now you have to."

Lauren blushed even redder and whispered so quietly that only Leah could hear her reply.

"I guess…Finley."

"What?" said Dawn.

"Who did you say?" asked Joy.

Before Lauren could repeat herself Joy's mother came down the steps. Everyone shushed each other and suppressed their giggles.

"Lights out, girls," Joy's mom said. "It's late. Turn off the TV and get some sleep."

Everyone murmured goodnight and settled into their blankets and pillows. After the coast was clear and they were alone again, Dawn whispered into the silence.

"How about another round of confession? This time everyone says their celebrity crush."

Everyone forgot about Lauren's answer and moved onto other topics until one by one they fell asleep. Suddenly, Leah felt a hand gently shake her awake.

"Leah?" Lauren whispered.

Leah stretched. "Hmm?"

"Um…about tonight—what we all said tonight—about our crushes…"

Leah quickly became more coherent at the word 'crushes' and propped herself up with her elbows. As surprised as she was at Joy for thinking she was dating Finley, she was equally surprised to hear someone had a crush on him. *Is Lauren going to ask for her help? Did she want her to become the middleman and see if Finn liked her back?* She dreaded what Lauren was going to say next.

She whispered, "Yeah?"

Lauren bit her lip nervously. "I know we all said we'd keep each other's secrets. But—"

Oh no, here it comes, thought Leah.

"Will you seriously not tell Finley about what I said?"

"What?"

"Don't tell him I like him," Lauren whispered hurriedly. "I know you two are friends and probably tell each other tons of stuff but I really don't want him to know."

Leah smiled in relief. "Yeah, of course. Your secret's safe with me."

Lauren's voice shook a little. "What about the others?"

Leah sat up straighter. "I don't think they heard. If they did, they would've said something earlier…and they probably would've suggested I set you guys up or something."

Lauren released a deep breath. Apparently, she was just as relieved as Leah.

"Thanks," she said.

"No problem." Leah smiled reassuringly, even though Lauren had gone back to her sleeping-bag and couldn't see it.

"So, what did you guys do after everyone left?" Finley asked Leah on Monday.

They were sitting in his tree house, deciding on a plan of attack for their summer list.

Leah shrugged. "We just hung out. We watched some TV, ate popcorn, talked about random stuff. What about you?"

"I fell asleep right away. I was exhausted." He took out a calendar and flipped through it. "OK, today's the last Monday of June, which means…" He counted the weeks. "We have nine weeks to complete everything. Easy. That's one thing per week."

Leah shook her head. "No, I'm going to my aunt and uncle's cabin during the first two weeks of August."

Finley looked up from the calendar. "Oh? I didn't know you were going to visit them."

"I only found out yesterday, after church. Apparently, my aunt and uncle were invited to some sort of business conference and asked my parents if we could watch over the place while they're gone.

You know, water their plants, make sure there's no tree damage from a storm, that kinda thing."

"Are you looking forward to it?"

"Not as much as our plans," Leah admitted, "but it might be kinda cool, as long as I don't get bored after the first three days."

Finley crossed off the two weeks of August with a pencil. "Then we're left with seven weeks to do everything. What do you want to do first?"

"Ice cream, definitely. It's starting to get super hot and I've been craving cookies and cream for days."

"I could go for some strawberry right about now." Finley smirked.

Leah looked at their list. "Some of these will require more planning. Hmm…I'll check around when a dance class is being offered."

"Yay," Finley mumbled sarcastically.

She ignored him. "The theater always shows horror movies during the last week of July. We'll probably find an R-rated one then."

"OK." He penciled in 'Movie?' on his calendar then said, "I think the rest is pretty easy to do whenever."

"Cool. Let's get some ice cream."

"Yeah." Finley wiped his sweaty hands on his shorts before climbing down the tree.

The sun blazed above their heads as they walked to the nearest convenience store. They could even feel heat radiating off the sidewalk and seeping through the bottoms of their sandals. Leah looked to the sky in wonderment. *Could I somehow paint the sun's fiery tentacles? Could I even find a color to depict the richness of the sun's heat?*

When they finally entered the store, a burst of cool air made the sweaty hairs on their arms stand up, as though in celebration.

"They have mint chocolate chip?" Finley said excitedly as he opened the cooler. "I'm getting that instead of strawberry. Hey, did you know vanilla is the most popular flavor of ice cream in the world?"

Leah shook her head. "No. Can you pass me a cookies and cream?"

"We should have brought spoons," Finley said as they made their way to the checkout.

She frowned in confusion. "Why?"

"This'll be half melted by the time we get to either of our houses. We could've eaten outside, right away, if we had spoons."

"Look, there are some by the slushie machine," Leah said.

"Is it OK if we take two spoons from there?" Finley asked the cashier.

She nodded. "Sure, go ahead. Take a napkin too, if you want."

Leah read her name tag. "Thank you, Beth."

"Yeah, thanks," Finley said and dropped his change into the tip jar.

"Hey guys." Lewis ran up to them with bags of licorice sticks loaded up in his arms. "What are the odds of seeing you here, huh?"

"Hi, Lewis," Finley replied.

"Wow, what are you doing with all that candy?" Leah asked.

Lewis laughed. "I'm stocking up for the summer. My stepdad convinced Mom to let us go camping so I'll need extra energy to walk the trails and go fishing and stuff."

"Sounds fun," Finley said.

"Plus, licorice makes the perfect straw once you bite the ends off," Lewis explained excitedly.

"I've never tried it," Leah said. "But it sounds–"

Lewis pointed at them. "Hey, it seems you guys are gonna have a sugar high, too."

She held up her pail of ice cream. "Oh, uh…"

Lewis shook his head sadly. "Of course, I can't bring that with. It would totally melt…but then I could drink it through a licorice straw. Wait, that's genius."

He ran to the coolers before Finley and Leah could say goodbye. They chuckled as they each grabbed a spoon then braved the outdoor heat again.

"Where do you want to eat?" Finley squinted at the bright sky.

"How about here?" Leah peeked into a little alleyway next to the store, which was for delivery trucks.

Finley asked, "Why here?"

Leah shrugged. "It's close and in the shade. Plus, people won't stare at us awkwardly while we each try eating a whole gallon of ice cream."

Finley laughed and sat on the cool pavement. "Good point."

Leah sat beside him then took off the lid. "Here goes."

"To the beginning of a great summer." Finley tapped his spoon against Leah's then loaded it with ice cream.

"So good." She smacked her lips and took another scoop.

"Mmm-hmm," he replied.

They dug into their sweet, creamy treats, talking very little in between scoops. Finley got brain freeze only once and when Leah's tub was about half empty she began slurping the melted portions. After ten minutes, they were already feeling stuffed.

"How much do you have left?" Leah asked.

Finley grunted and tilted his tub to reveal about a quarter of it was still full.

"I've got more." Leah showed her bucket. It still had about a third left.

"I'm so full, I don't know if I can do it…," he mumbled.

"You're so close though. Don't you want to finish?"

He grunted again and took another bite. "You've got to finish, too."

"I'm trying," she said and slurped another spoonful. "But I'm starting to feel sick."

"Yeah."

"Are you going to give up?"

Finley shook his head. "I—I'm going to do it."

Determinedly, he shoved another huge scoop into his mouth.

Leah encouraged him. "I think you just need to eat two more scoops and you'll be done."

Finley looked at her. Pain was reflected in his eyes and his face had a green tint, although it was hard to tell if that was from the sticky ice cream around his mouth or because he was feeling nauseous.

"Here." Leah wearily took his spoon and tub then stirred the ice cream until it had all melted. "Now there's less air in it. All you have to do is drink that last bit."

There was a little bubble in the minty, chocolatey puddle. It popped menacingly as Finley looked at it with disgust.

"Come on," Finn urged himself aloud. "I'll regret it if I don't finish. I can do it. I'm so close, I can do it."

He burped then brought the tub to his mouth. With eyes shut tight, he gulped down the remaining bit then lazily threw the tub across the alley.

"You did it," Leah exclaimed.

"Egh," he replied.

Leah patted his arm. "Wow, congrats. How do you feel?"

Finley's frown was all the answer she needed.

"Your turn." He motioned to her ice cream.

She took another scoop up to her lips then gagged and brought it down. Her eyes pleaded with his and she whispered, "Please don't make me do it."

Suddenly, Finley's whole body jerked. He quickly got up and ran to the other side of the dumpster so Leah couldn't see him but she could hear him. He'd thrown up. Twice.

Leah and Finn's List for an Awesome Summer

1. ~~Eat a whole gallon of ice cream (each)~~
2. Build a throne
3. Take a dance class
4. Hunt crabs at night, at the beach
5. Sneak into an R rated movie at the theater
6. Drive a car
7. Discover a new world
8. Stay awake for 24 hours straight
9. Find buried treasure
10. Attempt a world record

4

"Finn, I'm so sorry," Leah said again as they trudged back home.

"It's OK," Finley replied. "We both agreed to eat that much ice cream. It's not as though you forced it down my throat."

He gagged again and Leah held out her bucket in case he wanted to throw up in it.

"I'm good," he said, with a hand on his stomach.

"You can still brag that you finished it," Leah said encouragingly. "We don't have to tell people that afterwards you…you know."

Finley smirked. "You wanna know the grossest part?"

"What?"

"It was green."

"Your puke?"

He chuckled. "Yeah."

"Ew."

He chuckled again. "Yeah."

They stopped on the sidewalk in front of Leah's house, sticky with sweat and melted ice cream.

"Are you fine walking home by yourself?" she asked.

Finn nodded. "It's not far."

"Are you sure?"

"Yeah. I think I'll take a cold shower and veg out on the basement floor. It's the coldest part of the house."

"All right then, see you later."

"See you."

From the front door Leah shouted, "Call me when you feel better and we can check off another item on our list."

Finley gave a 'thumbs up' then lazily stumbled the last block home. His cold shower brought a stop to the burning sensation on his skin. In the basement, he surfed the TV channels with a can of ginger ale and a package of saltine crackers. It was an old trick his Mom had taught him to feeling better. Ginger did wonders for the stomach. He landed on the Home Shopping Network and was half an hour into an episode of "Magic Sponge: the only sponge that leaves the scent of lemon on every surface" when his mom came home.

"Here you are," she said, as she descended the stairs. "I was beginning to wonder if you were still playing with Leah."

Finley cringed. "We don't play, Mom. We hang out."

"Oh. Excuse me." She crossed her arms mockingly, as though insulted by her son's correction. "Anyway, your dad and I are planning on barbecuing tonight. Do you want a hot dog or a hamburger?"

Finley hesitated. He wasn't hungry but, also, didn't want to admit he'd been sick earlier. *She might ask questions and learn about the summer list. It's better as a secret. Besides, she'd stop me and Leah from doing some of the things on it. She'd never let us see an R-rated movie, for example.*

"*Hot dog.*" He thought, *It's less food than a hamburger. I can manage to eat it, right?*

"Do you want two, as usual?"

"Um…nah. Maybe I'll just eat more veggies or something."

His mom narrowed her eyes.

Uh-oh, he thought. *Now she's suspicious.*

"Are you feeling OK?" she asked, as she scanned the room and found his easy-on-the-stomach snack.

"Yeah," he replied quickly. "Yeah, it's just the heat's getting to me a little. I'm fine though."

She nodded slowly. "Maybe you should stay inside tomorrow. Enjoy the AC and stay cool. I don't want you getting heat exhaustion."

"OK."

"OK," she said and slowly ascended the stairs.

Finley sighed in relief. *That was too close. I'll have to be more careful in the future.*

"Hey," his mom called from the top of the stairs. "I forgot to ask, how's Leah doing?"

"She's fine. I think it's too hot for her as well."

"What did the two of you do today?"

Finley avoided eye contact by looking at the TV again. "Not much. Just hung out. Had some ice cream."

"Ah," she said knowingly, "so you filled up on ice cream, didn't you? That's why you're not hungry."

Finley looked back at her and knew he was in the clear. He shrugged. "I guess you caught me."

"Leah, is that you?"

"Yeah, Diane."

Leah found her sister sitting at the kitchen table, flipping through a magazine and sipping iced coffee through a straw. She glanced at Leah.

"What's with the ice cream pail?"

"It's nothing." Leah went to the sink to wash then recycle it.

Diane looked her up and down. "Ew, you're all wet. What were you doing? Running through the sprinklers again?"

"I haven't done that since I was...I dunno, ten."

"It isn't raining, is it?"

"No, I just walked home from the convenience store."

Diane lowered her magazine. "You walked all the way to Crocus Street?"

"Just to Cole Street."

"That's, like, four blocks away."

"I know."

"You sweated that much, just from walking eight blocks?"

"Well, Finn and I took a break and sat in the shade for a bit."

"Why? It's so hot. No one should be outside that long."

Leah sighed. The heat and her sister's condescending tone were getting on her nerves. She grabbed a bottle of water from the fridge and went to her room.

At five-thirty her dad knocked on her door, interrupting her reading.

"Your mom just pulled up on the driveway. Can you help her put away the groceries?"

"Sure, Dad."

"Unless you were doing homework," he explained. "You can finish that first."

Leah shook her head in confusion. "It's summer break now—"

"Oh, right," her dad said. "Sorry, I forgot. It was a crazy day at work."

"It's OK."

Leah watched him out of the corner of her eye as they unpacked. He'd been more forgetful lately and definitely stressed. When he smiled, his lips were too tight and his eyes didn't crinkle anymore. She wondered what was going on.

"Hey, Dad," she asked, "do you want to play a game of Hearts after supper?"

"I'm pretty tired tonight," he replied. "I think I'll watch the basketball game. Maybe tomorrow, OK?"

Leah nodded.

"I'll play," her mom offered. "Diane?"

She shrugged. "Why not? I don't have any other plans tonight anyway."

Diane won the most rounds that night, with their mom second and Leah in last place. The basketball announcers' voices kept pulling her concentration away from the game and toward her father. He was alone in the living room with glassy eyes and a lukewarm cola in his hand.

5

"I found a way for us to get to the beach tomorrow night," Finley told Leah.

She'd taken the phone to her room so no one would hear about her secret plans with him. "Tomorrow night? Are we going crab hunting?"

"Yep."

"How?"

"Bryce's brother Seth has a date at a restaurant close by. He'll give us a ride and we can walk to the beach from there."

Leah shook her head. "Why would he give us a ride? We're not his friends."

"Bryce owes me a favor for studying with him during finals. Anyway, I explained six hours of studying should make up for two fifteen-minute rides with his brother."

"You just explained why Bryce would help. Why would Seth?"

Finley chuckled. "Apparently, Bryce blackmailed him. He didn't say much, only he has some pretty juicy information about Seth. If he bails on us, Bryce will spill everything to their parents."

Leah smirked. "That's good enough for me, I guess. What time are we going?"

"Be ready to go at seven forty-five."

"Isn't that early? It'll still be light out."

"I know, but I couldn't make Seth drive us any later. He said if the date goes well, he'll meet us back at the restaurant at eleven. That'll give us about two hours to hunt crabs in the dark."

"What if the date's bad?"

"He'll find us on the beach and we'll have to leave early."

Leah inhaled sharply. "Hope it goes well then."

"We'll only have an hour to kill anyway. Maybe we can pick out some good spots in the meantime."

"All right."

"Great," replied Finn.

"I'll bring a flashlight and a pair of sneakers."

"I'll do the same. Do we need anything else?"

Leah suggested, "Maybe a shovel?"

"I'll take my mom's gardening spade. That'll work, right?"

She shrugged, even though he couldn't see her. "I don't see why not. I'll bring a pail to carry the crabs in."

"Perfect. See you tomorrow."

"My parents don't want me out past ten," she warned, "so make Seth park by the Andersons' house. I'll sneak out my bedroom window and meet you there."

"OK."

"Hey," Leah said as she got into the backseat of Seth's dirty, brown car.

"Got everything?" Finley asked.

"Yep."

"This is it, right?" Seth asked, "I don't have to pick up any more kids?"

Finn and Leah looked at one another; both were annoyed at being called a 'kid'.

"Yeah, let's go," Finley finally said.

"You'd think he'd clean up his car before a date," Leah murmured as she wiped her dusty hands on her shorts.

"I know, right?"

"Maybe he's too cheap to wash his car."

Finley smirked. "Maybe he's waiting for the rain to do it."

"Maybe everyone in the backseat should shut up," Seth exclaimed.

"Oops," Leah mouthed to Finn.

He paused then asked Seth, "Who's the lucky lady you're seeing tonight?"

Seth glared at him through the rear-view mirror. "What did I just say?"

"To shut up."

"So do it."

Finley was quiet and looked out the window. About five seconds later he asked, "Is she smart? Pretty? Is she more of a bookworm or athlete? Not that she has to be just one, of course. She could be both, for all I know. I guess what I want to know is…does she have a younger sister?"

Leah giggled but Seth's eyes bulged. After they pulled up to the restaurant he practically dragged Finley out of the car.

"Look," he said, "I'm only going to explain this once. You're coming with me to the beach and back home. That's it. If I see you anywhere near the restaurant before eleven, you're going to regret it. After my date's over, I can do whatever I want with you. So, if you want to see your mommy and daddy ever again, you'll shut up, walk away and pretend you don't know me until I take you home. Got it?"

Finley nodded, as though deeply pondering what Seth had said then asked, "What are you gonna eat? If I were you, I'd stay away from onion and garlic if you plan on kissing her later."

Seth hissed, "One word. Just say one more. I dare you."

Finn shrugged. He got his things out of the car then waved goodbye as he walked with Leah to the beach.

When they reached the sand, she asked, "Why'd you tease him so much? Aren't you going to regret it later?"

"Nah," Finn said nonchalantly. "Seth would never hurt me. He's actually a pretty nice guy. I've been at his house enough times to learn how to read him. When I'm playing video games with Bryce, sometimes he even joins us; but, when he's with his friends, he acts tough. I think tonight he was just nervous about his date."

"Are you sure?"

"Absolutely. By the time he picks us up, he'll have forgotten the whole thing."

"But what if his date goes badly and he gets us early?"

"The only way that'll happen is if the girl's terrible to him. Trust me, he's a gentleman with the ladies and a jerk with his friends."

Leah's forehead wrinkled. "If you say so. I'm just glad he's mad at you and not me."

"It's still pretty hot." Finley shaded his face from the sun. "What do you say we find some drinks and sit in the shade until it gets dark?"

"That's the best thing you've said all day."

They walked to the closest kiosk and picked up two cans of orange soda. Behind the clerk, an assortment of colorful souvenirs and beach gear were on display, from key chains to water wings.

Leah asked him, "When do you close?"

The clerk pointed at the operation of hours sign and smacked his bubblegum. "Thirty minutes."

Finley directed her attention to the fishing nets. "Do you think we'll need one of those?"

She shrugged. "I think we're fine with just using our bucket. Besides, things here are always overpriced. It's probably not worth it."

They found a free bench in the shade and sipped their sodas, as they commented on the other beachgoers.

"Look at that kid." Finley pointed to the water. "He's hilarious."

Leah squinted. "What's he doing?"

"I heard him yelling he's an octopus."

"Wait…isn't that Lewis?"

Finley looked harder. "Wow, I—I think you're right."

Lewis had taken three pool noodles into the water and was trying to keep afloat on top of them. He'd tucked one under his legs, another under his back and he slapped the water around him with the third. Meanwhile, a grandfather was chasing his granddaughter out of the water and inadvertently got smacked in the rear by him. The man yelped in surprise but Lewis didn't seem to notice what he'd done and kept on playing.

"I gotta admit, I admire his confidence to just be himself." Leah chuckled.

"Sometimes, I wish I had a brother." Finley sighed.

"Same." Leah nodded. "Having a sister is rough. Brothers must be so much easier."

Finn looked at her. "What do you mean?"

"Diane's always bossing me around and pretends to know everything when she doesn't and makes fun of me all the time."

"But brothers do that kind of stuff, too."

"Yeah but they wouldn't tell me what to wear to school or chase me around the house with a bottle of perfume and spray me over and over."

He smirked. "She does that?"

"Sometimes. Plus, adults wouldn't mix up my name if I had a brother. Every year some teacher calls me Diane for the first couple days of school. It's annoying being compared to her."

"Sounds kinda fun to me."

"It's not."

The sun was just about to fully dip below the horizon and only a small fraction of people were still around. Most of them were small groups of teens goofing off or couples taking photos together with the sunset.

"We could probably start looking for some good hunting spots," Leah said, as she stood up.

"Sure," Finley said, as he tossed their cans into a nearby bin. "How do we start?"

"I don't know. I thought you knew."

"No."

"Finn. Wasn't it your idea to hunt crabs at night?"

"I thought it was yours."

"No, when we were kids you said something about your cousins sneaking off to the beach and coming home with a crab. They told their parents the next day they'd bought it at a pet shop so they could keep it."

Finley shook his head. "Nuh-uh. When we were six or seven you watched it in a movie and said you wanted to try it someday."

"I never said that."

"Yes, you did."

"OK, stop." Leah held out her hands. "This isn't helping. Do you know anything about hunting for crabs?"

"Other than they like to hide in the sand? No. Do you?"

She shook her head.

"I guess we can find a hole and try to dig it out," he suggested.

"If you dig, I'll try to catch it with the bucket."

He held out his hand for a high-five. "Deal."

They walked up and down the sandy landscape, looking for holes where crabs could be hiding. It was very dark within minutes of the sunset and their flashlights cast strange shadows on the sand, making the search harder.

"It's so quiet," she whispered.

"Yeah," he whispered back. "It's weird to only hear the water and our feet in the sand."

"I like it. It's peaceful."

Finn tilted his flashlight toward his face and laughed maniacally.

Leah giggled at him.

"Wait." He flashed his light over a hole. "There's one."

"Yes."

He held his flashlight between his teeth and began to dig. Leah kept watch with her pail, ready to trap the crab as soon as it was uncovered.

"There it is." She squealed as the crab's head poked out of the hole then quickly scurried deeper into the sand.

"I saw it. OK, I'll scoop it out and dump it over here. Ready?"

"Uh-huh."

He carefully dumped his next shovelful of sand and the crab scuttled into sight. Leah gasped and lunged forward to trap it under her pail.

"We got it," she exclaimed.

Finn jumped up and down. "Let me see."

She slowly tilted the pail to unveil their prize. Nothing was there.

"Are you sure you caught it?" he asked.

"I thought so," Leah said and lifted the whole pail off the ground. It was empty. "It must have gotten away before I could catch it."

"That's all right, it couldn't have gone far." He flashed his light around but they couldn't find the crab.

"Sorry, Finn."

"We'll find more," he said, encouragingly.

They scoured the sand for several minutes before Leah saw something. She pointed her flashlight to another hole.

"There."

"OK." Finn repositioned himself and began to dig. This one was close to the surface and Leah caught it under her pail immediately.

"I definitely got it this time." She beamed and slowly lifted the pail. Again, there was nothing in it.

"I saw you catch it," he said, baffled by the disappearance. "Where did it go?"

"Oh." Leah smacked her head with her palm. "Duh. It buried itself back in the sand."

Finley looked at her for a moment then they burst out laughing.

"We're so dumb. Of course they're disappearing." He clutched his side.

"I can't believe it took us two tries to figure it out." Leah gasped for breath.

"It's probably still here." He nudged the ground with his shoe. The sand shook slightly then settled.

"Just get it onto your shovel," she prompted.

He scooped a chunk of sand and softly shook some of the excess off. There appeared to be a rock perched in the center of his spade but then it grew legs and moved.

"Quick, grab it and put it in the pail," he whispered excitedly.

"I'm not touching that thing. It'll pinch me. I'll take the shovel and you pick it up."

"No way. Here, I'll just dump it all into your pail."

The crab seemed unbothered as it nestled itself deeper into the sand in Leah's pail. Fascinated, they watched the crab, on their hands and knees.

"I've never seen one this close before," Leah whispered.

"I've eaten them and seen them in grocery stores but I've never seen them up close in their habitat," Finley remarked.

"I want to touch the shell. Where are its pincers?"

He pointed. "Here."

Leah moved toward the back of the crab and gently stroked its back. "It's cold," she marvelled. "I wonder if that's because the sand's cooler at night. Do you think they're warm during the day?"

Finley shrugged. "Maybe."

"Hey, buddy," she said to the crab. "You're gorgeous and I like the color of your shell."

"I heard a Japanese spider crab can live up to a hundred years."

Leah's eyebrows raised. "What?"

"Yeah, it was on a cartoon show."

"You remember the weirdest facts, dude."

"They're not weird, they're cool. Anyway, what should we do with the crab now?" Finley asked. "Do you want to keep it?"

"No. I just wanted to see if we could catch one. Do you want it?"

"Nah. I can't keep it alive as a pet and I'm not gonna eat it." The subject of food suddenly reminded him of Seth at the restaurant. "Hey, what's the time anyway?"

Leah checked her watch. "Ten minutes to eleven. We should probably head back to the restaurant." She brushed the shell with her fingertips one last time and whispered, "Time to let you go."

She carefully emptied the pail's contents then watched in delight as the crab burrowed until it was out of sight.

"That's so cool." He grinned.

"Got all your tools and stuff?"

"Yep. Let's bounce."

Seth was waiting outside his car as they approached, listening to some cheesy, generic song on the radio.

Finn jokingly punched his arm. "So…? How'd it go?"

"It was fine." Seth shrugged but couldn't hide his goofy grin. "What about you?"

"Fine." Leah grinned at Finn.

"You're not even giving your date a ride home?" Finley teased.

Leah and Finn's List for an Awesome Summer

1. ~~Eat a whole gallon of ice cream (each)~~
2. Build a throne
3. Take a dance class
4. ~~Hunt crabs at night, at the beach~~
5. Sneak into an R rated movie at the theater
6. Drive a car
7. Discover a new world
8. Stay awake for 24 hours straight
9. Find buried treasure
10. Attempt a world record

6

"Did anyone realize you snuck out of the house yesterday?" Leah asked Finley on the phone.

"Nope. You?"

"No, I crawled through my window undetected."

"Nice. Wanna hang out today?"

"Mom wants to take Diane and me shopping for some extra summer clothes. We've outgrown a bunch of ours from last year and I'm too skinny to fit into Diane's hand-me-downs. What about Sunday afternoon?"

"Works for me. We can talk more about the next thing to do on our summer list."

"Leah, let's go," Diane called from the front door. "Mom's already waiting in the car."

"Gotta go. See you tomorrow, Finn."

"Bye."

Leah grabbed her bag off the kitchen counter and ran to the car. Diane had already taken the front passenger seat so she slid into the back among their boxes of old clothes.

"Ready?" her mom asked.

Leah nodded. "Yep. Where are we going first?"

"We'll drop off your clothes at the thrift store then head over to the outlet mall."

"Can we go to that store from last year?" Diane asked. "I don't remember the name… Warehouse something or Garage-town thingy…"

"I know the one you're talking about," Mrs. Harris laughed. "And yes, we can. Their prices are reasonable enough. What about you, Leah? Anywhere specific you want to go?"

Leah shrugged. "Nah. Why don't we just look for stuff at the thrift store while we're there?"

"I don't think you'll find anything that fits you anymore," her mom explained. "You've grown a lot this past year and most of the clothes at this thrift store are for children. The one on the opposite end of town has adult clothing but it's far out of our way. Is there a store close by you want to visit?"

"Nah, any place that sells shorts is fine."

Diane looked back at her. "You're not only getting shorts, are you?"

"I like shorts," Leah said, defiantly.

"But there are so many options for girls. We can wear dresses, skirts, overalls—"

"Those are all harder to do stuff in. I want to run or sit with my legs spread out. I can't do that in a skirt."

"You can in overalls," Diane argued.

"But then I have to practically take everything off when I need to pee."

"Fine," she relented. "If you want to just wear the same boring stuff all the time, don't take my advice."

"I won't," Leah mumbled.

"Girls," their mother broke in. "I was thinking it would be nice if we picked up something for your father today. He's been working very hard these past few months and—"

Leah interrupted, "Why is that, Mom?"

"Yeah." Diane joined in, "He never wants to do anything anymore. He's always so tired."

Mrs. Harris explained, "About three months ago, a new company bought the business your dad works for. It's called a business acquisition. They want the business to be run differently to make more money. In doing so, they've changed a lot of things; they've made new work rules and schedules, they've even gotten rid of some jobs. Your father has lost a few co-workers lately because of it."

"Are they going to fire Dad?" Diane asked and Leah's eyes grew wide.

"No," their mom reassured them. "We're confident he'll stay employed because he does so much of their financial paperwork but he's been under a lot of pressure to work faster than he's used to."

"That's not fair," Leah said indignantly. "If the business is already making money, they shouldn't have to work harder."

Her mother sighed. "I agree, some people aren't satisfied with a little success, though. They want much more and, sadly, that often means sacrifices have to be made."

Leah frowned. "Sacrifices?"

Her mom elaborated, "Working long hours, taking short breaks, pushing people to work harder and faster for the same amount of wages."

"Can they really do that?" Diane asked. "Make people work harder for the same pay at the end of the week?"

"Unfortunately, yes. There are many people in the world without a job and would gladly have one similar to your father's. People do astounding things to provide for their families."

The car was silent for a moment, as each passenger considered the situation.

"That's sad," Leah finally said.

"Yes, it is," her mom agreed.

"What can we do to help?" Diane asked.

Their mom smiled sadly. "I'm trying to figure that out, too."

"We can have a party," Diane suggested. "An 'Appreciate Dad' party."

Mrs. Harris pondered the idea. "Interesting…"

"We can get some balloons," Leah said, excitedly.

"And it'll just be us," Diane continued, "so there aren't too many people and we'll do all of Dad's favorite things."

"We can make a cake." Leah beamed.

"And get pizza and cola," their mother added. "Yes, I think it's a very nice idea."

"Can we do it tomorrow, after church?" Diane asked. "It'll be a huge surprise."

"I don't see why not." Their mom laughed.

"I'll start making a list of things we need." Diane took out a pen and pad of paper from the glove-box. "This is going to be such a good weekend. Shopping today and partying tomorrow."

Finn picked up the ringing telephone. "Hello?"

"Hey, Finn, it's Leah again. Sorry but I'm gonna have to cancel our plans for tomorrow. My family decided we needed to spend a day together."

"Is everyone all right?"

"Yeah, we're OK. Dad's been working hard lately so the rest of us decided it'd be good to show him some extra love."

"Oh, that's nice," Finley remarked. He knew she wouldn't have cancelled if it wasn't important so he let her off the hook easily. "Enjoy your time together. Want to meet up on Monday instead?"

"Yeah, I was thinking maybe we should try beating a world record next. We could go to the library and see if they have a book on world records from last year."

"I'll drop by your place around nine, sound good?"

"Works for me and sorry again about tomorrow."

"No problem. Really."

"Bye."

"Later, 'gater."

He hung up the phone, strolled to the kitchen, grabbing a juice box and granola bar. It looked as if it were going to rain later in the afternoon, which made it the perfect day to be a couch potato. In the basement, he took out all his favorite video games and piled them in front of the TV. He scanned them with glee before making his selection then settled down on the floor with a large blanket.

He grinned mischievously and said to himself, "Now, it's time for some brain-numbing fun."

Two hours later, he'd beaten his *Super Mario Bros.* high score.

Wow. He shook his head to clear the cobwebs of intense concentration. *Maybe I should take a break.* He sank into the couch cushions and surfed the TV channels. *No. No. Maybe. Ew, why are there so many soap operas on?*

His dad came down the stairs. "Hey, buddy. What are you doing?"

Finley twisted around to face him. "Nothing much."

"I'm going on a quick grocery run before it starts to rain. Want to join me?"

"No, thanks. I'm kinda tired now."

"Oh? Did you sleep OK last night?"

"Yeah. I just beat a video game high score, that's all."

"I see," his dad said in disinterest. "OK then, I guess I'll take off by myself."

"Bye." Finn turned back to the TV and kept flipping until he found a cartoon show. It was a little juvenile for him but he figured it was better than nothing. Besides, he was too lazy to put a tape in the VHS player. Half an hour later he was dozing peacefully on the couch, unaware of the rain pattering against the window panes.

7

The church sermon on Sunday morning seemed especially appropriate to Leah. The pastor talked about having an attitude of humility while serving others; but, as relevant he was, her mind kept drifting back to the party plans she'd made with her sister and mom. Yesterday, after they'd purchased some new summer clothes, they picked up an ice cream cake, they figured it was sneakier to buy one and hide it in the freezer than make their own. Next, they picked up some balloons, streamers and rented the movie *Honey I Shrunk the Kids*. The father in the movie always made Mr. Harris laugh and he enjoyed teasing Diane and Leah about it. Unlike the kids in the movie, he didn't think his daughters would survive being the size of an ant.

Leah's attention was brought back to the service when she noticed everyone stand up and get ready to sing. Diane was a part of the worship team that day so Leah already knew the words to the songs. She'd heard Diane practicing all week and always noticed a difference in her sister when she sang worship songs. At no other time would her face show as much peace and joy as it did then; sometimes her eyes would glisten with tears. Once Leah asked her about it but Diane pretended it didn't happen and changed the subject.

"Let us go forth and serve one another in humility this week," the pastor concluded.

Diane met them in the foyer and gave her mom a secretive wink when her dad wasn't looking. Leah knew that meant the next phase of their plan was in progress. When they got home, Diane looked around the car.

"Oh," she pretended to be upset. "I left my purse at church. Can we go back and get it?"

"Are you sure it's not with you?" their dad asked.

"Yes." Diane nodded vigorously. "I know exactly where it is, too."

"Why don't you go," their mom suggested. "Leah and I will start working on lunch."

"OK," their dad agreed. "Come sit up front with me, Diane."

She beamed. "Thanks, Dad."

Leah and her mom waved goodbye as the car left the driveway then giggled and rushed to the door.

"We have about half an hour before they're back," her mom said. "We'll have to hurry."

"Last night I blew up some balloons and stuffed them into my closet," Leah mentioned. "I just have to hang them and the streamers up."

"Good thinking, Leah. I'll order the pizza then help you decorate."

They'd split off to do their individual tasks and were just putting the pizza on the table when the car pulled up.

"They're here, they're here." Leah bounced.

"Open the door for them," her mother said, eagerly.

She waited until they were right at the door then threw it open and yelled, "Surprise."

Leah, Diane and their mother all rushed to give Mr. Harris a giant hug.

He grinned as he observed the decorations. "What's all this?"

Diane laughed. "We got you."

"Our daughters thought we should have a party, in your honor."

"But…but why?" Mr. Harris looked confused. "Is today a special day?"

"No," Mrs. Harris explained, "but you are special."

Leah added, "We just wanted to do something that'll make you happy."

Diane nodded. "You work so hard, Daddy, and we appreciate it."

"We appreciate you." Mrs. Harris smiled.

"Thank you." He wiped his eyes as he gazed lovingly at his family. His eyes stopped on Diane. "You left your purse on purpose, didn't you?"

She laughed. "You caught me."

They cheerfully sat down at the table and the room was as full of love as it was with the scent of warm pizza.

"Finley, are you there?"

Mr. Davidson peeked around the corner and found his son munching on a bowl of cereal in front of the living room TV.

"Mmm, hmm," Finn replied.

"When you're done eating, do you mind helping me with the dishes? I want to have them done before your mother comes home."

"What's she doing?"

"Just running a few errands. Filling up the car with fuel, that sort of thing. Will you be done soon?"

Finley gulped the last of the milk from his bowl then said, "Yes but can I finish this show first?"

"How much longer will it be?"

"About five minutes."

"OK." His dad retreated.

Mr. Davidson had just finished filling the sink with hot water and soap when Finley entered the room. He put his bowl and spoon on the counter, next to the other dirty dishes.

"I already put away the clean dishes from the dishwasher," his dad said. "You can put those in."

Finn obeyed his request.

"Thank you, Finley. Now you can dry and put away these dishes I'm washing now."

"Why don't we just let them air dry and put them away later?"

"Because I'd like you to help me," his dad explained. "I already emptied the dishwasher and started washing the remaining dirty dishes so this is the last job."

Finley frowned slightly. *Am I in trouble for something? Dad seems angry...maybe he just wants to talk.*

Mr. Davidson scrubbed at a stubbornly dirty fry pan. "What are some of your plans for the summer?"

"Um..." Finley searched for an answer his father would find approving. "Leah and I are going to the library tomorrow."

His dad looked at him in surprise. "Are you taking part in an extracurricular summer program?"

"No. We just want to look at some old world records. They're interesting."

"Yes, they can be. What else are you planning to do?"

Finley shrugged. "I dunno. Relax at home and hang out with my friends." His dad nodded but Finn sensed he wasn't satisfied with the answer. "Leah and her family are staying at a cabin next month. I'm not sure what I'll do then."

"You can always find something to do around the house," his father suggested. "For instance, I'd appreciate it, if you mowed the lawn today."

Finley thought to himself, *More chores? Why do I have to do them?*

Mr. Davidson caught a glimpse of his son's disapproval. "No need to frown. I just think you're old enough to help out more around here, especially because you're not busy."

Finley was raised to not argue with his parents or show disrespect so he sighed and nodded his head in defeat.

"Thank you, Finley."

Finn muttered to himself as he cut the grass. "It's not fair. I only have two months of summer vacation and Dad puts me to work. I already have a ton of stuff to do at school, plus homework. Now I'm being used as manual labor? For nothing; I'm not even getting paid for this. It's so unfair." He maneuvered his way around a tree and ducked under one of its branches. "Dad probably wants the TV to himself. That's why he made me come out here. With Mom and me out of the house, he can do whatever he wants." He quickly finished the front and back yard, sweating from the effort and the heat of the day. He put the lawnmower back in the garage then stared at a small section of grass he intentionally missed. He sneered. "You can make me cut the grass but you can't make me do a good job."

When he entered the house, he was careful not to make too much noise. He grabbed a bottle of water from the fridge, closed the door gently then snuck to his bedroom.

Now I'm safe from doing more chores, he thought. *If Dad looks for me, I'll just hide under the bed.* He grabbed a comic book and flopped onto his mattress. *Besides, I can easily pass the time in here.*

8

"Egh." Finn said, as Leah opened her front door. "Why did we agree to meet so early today?"

Leah chuckled. "I don't know. You're the one who suggested 9 o'clock. I figured you were busy in the afternoon so we had to meet early."

He yawned. "I don't know what I was thinking."

"At least it's not too hot right now."

He frowned to clearly show his disapproval of her optimism. "Let's just go."

Leah curled her fingers and stretched out her thumb and pinky. Holding her hand to her ear, she pretended to speak on the phone. "Hello? One moment, please." She pretended to cover the phone's mouthpiece and said, "Excuse me, Mr. Cranky-pants? There's a call for you on line one. It's the Grinch."

"Ha. Ha." Finn raised his hand to her face. "Talk to the hand."

"Excuse me, Mr. Hand? There's a call for—"

"Stop." Finn laughed in exasperation.

"Ah, now you're in a better mood." Leah smiled.

He changed the subject. "How was your family day?"

"It was great. We had pizza and ice cream cake for lunch then watched a movie, played a few board games and had pizza again for supper."

"What? I wanna have pizza for two meals in a row."

"It's Dad's favorite food," Leah explained. "And because yesterday was all about him, he chose to have it twice; no one argued."

"What kind of pizza?"

"Pepperoni then Meat-Lovers, both with extra cheese."

He licked his lips. "Mmm."

"Careful not to drool on the books." Leah pointed at the library across the street. "Let's cross here."

Inside, they were greeted with a waft of cool air and the earthy scent of paper.

"Where do we start?" Leah asked.

"I dunno. It's a lot bigger than our school library." Finley eyed a display of graphic novels. "I should come here more often, though."

"Me too." She ran her hand along an aisle of books as they passed by. "Maybe we should look in the history section?"

"That makes sense to me."

They drifted past overstuffed chairs, reading desks and a colorful floor mat in the children's section.

"Hi, Lauren." Leah waved.

Lauren was sitting in a large, padded chair by the window. Leah's voice had startled her and she almost dropped her book.

"Oh, hi, Leah," she said as she sat straighter. "Hi, Finley."

"Hey, Lauren. What are you reading?" Finley glanced over to read the title. "*The Count of Monte Cristo*?"

She nodded shyly. "It's very interesting."

Finley whistled. "That's a huge book."

Leah asked, "I haven't seen you here before. Do you come a lot?"

Lauren nodded. "I didn't used to but, lately, I've been coming often to read or do homework. It's hard to concentrate at home since my baby brother was born."

"What are your other plans for summer?" Finley asked.

Lauren's cheeks turned slightly pink. "This is it. I can read all the books I want in summer."

"You'll probably have the most exciting vacation out of all our classmates," Finley reasoned, "because you'll go on tons of adventures with the characters you read about."

She nodded.

Finley shrugged. "Anyway, Leah and I were gonna find a book of our own."

"Maybe we'll see you around?" Leah smiled. "We were just saying we should come here more often."

"Bye." Lauren waved.

Leah and Finley made their way deeper into the library.

"I wonder how long it takes to dust all of these books," Finn whispered.

"Maybe all day?"

He stifled a laugh. "Can you imagine? Dusting and holding your nose all day so you don't sneeze in a quiet library?"

"Here's the history section." Leah ducked into an aisle.

Together they scanned, Leah on one side, Finley on the other. Their eyes passed books that were large, small, plain, decorative and of all colors but mostly brown.

"Leah, did you know the Library of Congress is the world's largest library?" Finley said, his nose inches away from a large history book he'd pulled from the shelves.

"Finn," she groaned. "I thought you were helping me…"

"You're right." He put the book back. "The cover made it look interesting so I got distracted."

She paused. "Do you mean large as in the building is big? Or it has the most items in it?"

"The last one."

"Cool."

Half an hour passed with no results.

"This is taking forever," Finn whined, as he massaged his neck. "I'm starting to get a headache from craning my neck to read the titles."

"There must be an easier way to find what we're looking for. Why don't we ask a librarian for help?"

"Yes," he agreed emphatically. "Anything is better than this."

They walked over to the main desk but no one was there.

"Maybe she's stacking books?" Leah suggested.

He read the golden nameplate in the center of the desk. "Mrs. Kowalski."

"Yes, dear?" a woman asked from behind.

Leah shrieked and they both spun around.

"I'm sorry to have surprised you," the aged lady said. "I suppose I'm used to being quiet as I walk in a library."

"Yeah." Finn exhaled deeply. "I didn't hear you at all."

The librarian smiled. "How may I assist you?"

"We're looking for a book about world records," he replied.

"From 1992, specifically," Leah added.

"Off the top of my head, I can't recall seeing a book of that nature. I'll check our records." Mrs. Kowalski moved behind her desk and clicked something on her large, clunky computer. "This may take a while; please feel free to continue browsing in the meantime. I'll find you when I'm done."

"Thank you," Leah said as she and Finn made their way to the juvenile fiction section.

"I hope she finds one," he said, as they surveyed the books.

"Oh, look, Nancy Drew. Diane used to read these all the time."

"No, look at this one." Finn took a book off the shelf, *Ghosts, Ghouls and Goblins: Scary Short Stories*. We should read this one when we stay up all night."

"Good idea. Let's get it checked out."

The librarian noiselessly approached. "I'm sorry but we don't have any books about world records from 1992; however we do possess one from 1989, if you're interested."

Leah regarded Finn, as though reading his thoughts. "Thanks for looking but I don't think it'll have information that's recent enough for us."

The librarian nodded understandingly. "May I be of any further assistance?"

"We'll take this one," Finn said, as he handed her the scary storybook.

Mrs. Kowalski read the title. "Interesting choice. It's fascinating to me that most people read a story and leave the characters within its pages at the end of the day. Yet, with a scary story, the characters come to life and remain hidden in the shadows, even after we finish reading the words 'The End'." She signed out the book under Finn's library account. "Enjoy your adventure."

They left the library feeling both productive and unproductive.

"Now what do we do?" Leah asked. "How are we going to beat a world record if we don't even know what the records are?"

"I dunno know," he replied. "Do you think hat's how others do it?"

"What do you mean?"

"When other people want to beat a world record, do you think they look up what the old record was? Or do they just try to be the best at something?"

"Hey, maybe you're onto something," Leah said, as she absentmindedly waved to one of her neighbors. "We don't necessarily need to know what a record is to beat it. If we're creative enough, maybe we can be the first to hold a new kind of record."

"Hmm…we'll need to prove we did it. Wait." He stopped in his tracks. "Leah, what if we videotape ourselves?"

"Video proof. Good idea, Finn, and I think we should try to set multiple records, in case someone else has already done it."

"Yes. We'll just do our best at being the fastest, strongest, most talented or…whatever we need to be."

Leah's level of excitement matched his, as she followed him into the tree house.

Together they compiled a list of twelve records to set but after further discussion they settled on four (the others were either impractical or impossible to complete). Next, they divided a list of items to get, including the camcorder Leah's parents purchased on Boxing Day last year. Lastly, they agreed to meet back at the tree house the following morning to execute their plan.

World Records to Attempt:

1. Eat as many jelly beans in one minute as possible. With chopsticks.
2. Unravel a roll of toilet paper as fast as possible.
3. Eat as many saltine crackers as you can in one minute. No water allowed.
4. Do the most jumping jacks you can.

9

"Did you get everything?" Leah asked as she approached the tree house.

Finn beamed. "You bet I did. We're equipped to the max."

He'd set up a folding table and chair next to the tree house. A large bowl of jelly beans sat in the center.

Leah nodded her approval. "I've got a whole empty tape we can record on so we don't have to worry about running out and accidentally missing anything."

He rubbed his hands together. "I'm so excited. I hope we actually pull this off. Imagine what everyone at school would say if we came back holding a world record certificate."

"We'd probably stand out from the crowd of high school freshmen." Leah frowned, unsure if she wanted the attention. "I think I'd rather hang mine in my room than show it off at school…and it would be cool to be better than Diane at something; but wait, we agreed to not tell anyone about our summer list."

"Oh yeah…" He crossed his arms. "I hadn't thought of that."

"We'd be in the newspaper, a world record book and probably the news on TV."

"But we wouldn't need to worry about that book being in our library. It'd be too new." Finn chuckled. "Anyway, why worry about what might happen? Let's just do our thing, have fun and if we break a record, cool. If not, our secret's safe."

Leah nodded. "Yeah…you're right."

He looked down at the bowl of candy on the table. "Can I go first? I want to try the jellybean one."

"Sure. Just let me get the camcorder ready."

Finley was practically shaking with excitement. "No problem. Hey, do you think I should sit at the table or stand? I think I'll sit. Then I won't have to move the chopsticks as much from the bowl to my mouth. I didn't have time to practice yesterday but it can't be that hard," he babbled.

Leah positioned herself opposite Finn and held up the camcorder. She pushed a button to display the time so she could film and monitor when a minute had passed by, at the same time.

"OK. I'm ready to start filming. Are you ready?"

He looked down at the glass bowl, sparkling in the sunlight and full of rainbow-colored candy. To him, it was a treasure chest, full of glittering jewels waiting to be plucked by chopsticks, no less.

"Count me down," he commanded.

She pushed the record button and counted. "Three, two, one, go."

Finn shoved his chopsticks into the bowl of jelly beans and pinched them together. The smooth candy coating was slipperier than he'd expected and it took almost the whole minute for him to finally capture one.

"That's time." Leah stopped recording and slid the camera off her shoulder. "Want to do it again?"

"Yeah, I think I have the hang of it now."

They repeated their process; Leah filmed and Finley struggled to bring a bean to his mouth. This time he managed to eat three.

"One more time," he insisted after the minute was up. "Please, Leah."

"Fine," she said with a sigh, "but then I want a turn."

Forty seconds into his last attempt, he suddenly dropped the chopsticks. "Ah, my hand is cramping."

"OK, my turn." She instructed him on how to operate the camcorder then took her spot at the table.

Finley aimed the camera at her. "Ready?"

"Yes."

He pushed the red record button. "Three, two, one, go."

Full of determination and intense focus, Leah maneuvered the chopsticks and managed to eat four in a minute. She attempted three more times and set the record at seven jelly beans.

"That's probably the best I can do," she said as she grabbed a handful of beans and began effortlessly popping them into her mouth. "Do you want to try again?"

"No, I don't think I can beat seven. Let's try the next thing on the list."

"My hand could use a break before I try the toilet paper one. Let's skip to the cracker challenge."

He agreed and placed a whole package of saltine crackers in front of her. "It's your turn to go first."

She attempted to eat as many as possible in one minute, without the help of a glass of water. She got to four crackers.

"Are you kidding me?" Finley laughed at the end of her turn. "Why'd you stop eating?"

Leah tried to respond through the mashed cracker in her mouth but Finn couldn't understand her. She ran to the house, helped herself to a cup of water and came back out.

"My mouth is dry," she explained.

"So you could only eat four crackers? No way is it that bad."

"No?" Leah grabbed the camera from his hands. "Then prove it."

He tried. He shoved seven in his mouth at one time but couldn't swallow before the minute was up.

"See?" Leah insisted, "It's harder than it looks."

"Mmmmrrrrahhhh." Finley coughed cracker crumbs everywhere.

"I can't understand you with food in your mouth." Leah smirked.

He ran inside and drank his own glass of water before returning. "OK, let's just give up on that world record. It's way too hard."

"We can try the toilet paper one now."

They agreed and, for the first time in their lives, walked into the bathroom together.

Finley looked at Leah out of the corner of his eye. "Hey, while we're here…um…maybe you can explain something."

"What?"

"Why do girls go to the bathroom together?"

She rolled her eyes and replied matter-of-factly, "Mostly so they can gossip."

"Why don't you talk outside the bathroom?"

"Because the people we're gossiping about are less likely to hear, especially if they're boys."

"Huh."

She brought the subject back to the toilet paper. "I think we can approach this two ways. We can unroll this way…" She demonstrated by spinning the roll upward. "Or we can unroll this way…" She repositioned the roll then spun it downward. "Do you have a preference?"

"Um…upward?"

"OK then, I'll spin downward. Maybe one'll be faster than the other. Is it OK, if I go first again?"

"Go for it."

She raised her hands up to the roll, ready to strike. "Give me a countdown."

"Three, two, one, go."

Leah's hands flew, as she stroked the toilet paper, unraveling it with the same energy as a cat with a ball of yarn. The paper flew everywhere, covering half the floor and draping over her arms and legs. The mess was so ridiculous, she found herself laughing really, really hard despite her arms growing sore. She finished the roll after seventeen seconds.

She gasped for breath. "I don't know if it was record-breaking fast but it was fun."

They untidily rewrapped the roll onto the cardboard cylinder and exchanged it with a new one for Finley.

"OK, your turn to make a mess." She giggled, as she aimed the camera at him.

Toilet paper flew even crazier as he completed his turn. It covered the floor, toilet seat and somehow managed to string itself across the light fixture above the mirror. Leah had to keep pulling the paper off the camera so the view wasn't blocked and knew the video would be shaky from all of her laughter. Finn finished in twelve seconds then collapsed to the cold, tile floor. They were both laughing so much it took five minutes to calm down enough to speak.

Leah clutched her side. "This is one of the silliest things we've ever done."

"Wait, wait, wait." Finley was wheezing from laughter as he grabbed a clump of toilet paper and draped it over his head. "I'm ready for the trial, congresswoman."

She laughed so hard she didn't even make a sound. Her lungs were practically bursting by the time she could manage a gasp of air. "Even if this one doesn't break a record," she finally managed to say, "it was worth it."

"This is my favorite one yet. My stomach hurts from laughing."

It took them another five minutes to fully settle down and clean up their mess.

"Where should I put this?" Leah asked, as she held up her rerolled toilet paper.

"On the counter's fine. We'll use it."

"What are you going to say when your parents ask why they're rolled up so messily?"

He shrugged. "Whatever. I'll figure something out."

They made their way back outside for their final challenge.

Leah set the camera on the table and asked, "What's the last thing again?"

"We have jumping jacks left," he replied.

"Phew." Leah wiped her forehead. "Let's hurry up and finish before we both melt."

They decided to attempt their jumping jacks challenge together; it would be more fun and they could get out of the hot sun sooner. Finn guzzled down two glasses of water as they finalized the details.

"I'm not gonna bother counting aloud," Leah said. "We can do that when we re-watch the video."

Finley nodded in agreement as she pushed the record button. They stood side by side, facing the camera. Even though the large oak tree provided some shade, it did little to relieve them of the summer heat.

They counted off together, "Three, two, one, go."

They kept the same rhythm, up, down, up, down, for several minutes but Finley quickly began to feel unwell.

"I shouldn't have drunk so much water before we started," he said. "I've got a cramp in my side."

"You can't stop now," she reprimanded. "We just started."

"Yeah." He inhaled sharply. "You're right."

They kept going. Up, down, up, down. Suddenly, he stopped and grabbed his side.

"No, I can't do it. I have to stop."

"But—"

"Keep going, Leah. You can do this."

She didn't admit she wasn't feeling unwell, too. The sun felt as though it was cooking her from the inside out and the exercise definitely wasn't helping.

Finley chanted every time she jumped, "Go. Go."

"I—I don't feel good," she moaned after another minute.

"You're doing great. Don't give up."

She was starting to feel lightheaded and the world was tilting to one side.

"I have to—" She stopped and fell to the ground.

"Whoa, Leah." Finley came to her side. "Are you all right?"

"Water," she managed to say, between breaths.

Finn ran inside to grab a cold water bottle and wet towel. When he came back a minute later, he put the towel on her forehead and let her drink.

"Just sip it," he coached. "If you chug, you might puke it back up."

She did as instructed.

"Let's go sit in the basement where it's cooler," he suggested and helped her to her feet. "Oh, wait." He dashed to the camera and stopped it from recording any more. With the camera in one hand and Leah clinging to his other arm, they made their way inside. They sat on the cold floor and rested for about an hour.

"Thanks," Leah said as she took her second orange juice box from Finley.

"You're welcome and finish all your potato chips," he said.

"So, I had heat exhaustion?"

"I'm pretty sure, yeah."

"How do you know?"

"Remember last summer when my family went camping?"

She nodded.

"One day was super-hot but I was bored hanging around the campsite and wanted to explore a little. So I went for a walk along the trails. Mom told me to bring a water bottle but I forgot and wasn't wearing a hat or staying in the shade. Anyway, I got heat exhaustion and had the same symptoms you did. I was sweating a ton but my skin was cold; I felt weak, dizzy and had a headache. Thankfully, a couple strangers saw I wasn't looking too good and helped me back to our site. Dad got me to cool off in the car with the AC running."

"Why do I have to eat the snacks, though?"

"The sugar from the juice and potassium and salt from the chips helps our bodies fix themselves. Drinking tons and tons of water isn't actually the best thing to do…funny, huh?"

"Do you think this feels the same as having a migraine?" Leah winced.

He smiled. "I don't ever want to find out."

After they both felt better, Leah suggested they cleaned up the rest of their stuff still outside, in case Finley's parents showed up from work and asked what they'd been doing. Their bowl of jelly beans had become a large, hard mass after melting in the sun. They picked away at it as they watched the footage of their video and laughed all over again at the toilet paper challenge. When they got to the jumping jacks, they counted how many they completed. Finn had done 192 and Leah did 370 before she crumpled to the ground. Watching herself fall made her feel a little queasy again.

"Hey, Finn, thanks again for helping me. It's kinda embarrassing that I almost fainted."

He shrugged. "Sure thing; besides, I think we're even now."

"Huh?"

"With me puking and you almost fainting…I think we've had enough embarrassment for the summer."

The next day they mailed their videotape, along with a brief letter explaining who they were and how the judges could contact them if they achieved any world records. They were mature enough to know their video submission was a long shot but there was a spark of hope, an excitement at the possibility of being the best at something; even if it was something ridiculous.

Leah and Finn's List for an Awesome Summer

1. Eat a whole gallon of ice cream (each)

2. Build a throne

3. Take a dance class

4. Hunt crabs at night, at the beach

5. Sneak into an R rated movie at the theater

6. Drive a car

7. Discover a new world

8. Stay awake for 24 hours straight

9. Find buried treasure

10. Attempt a world record

10

Leah and Finley woke up at eight on Friday morning so they'd be in sync as they stayed awake for twenty-four hours straight. After it got dark, they secretly met at the tree house.

"What did you bring?" Finn asked.

Leah settled down on the floor, sitting cross-legged and thinking to herself how wrong Diane was to recommend wearing a skirt once in a while. She pulled out everything from her bag: gummy worms, peanut butter and chocolate cups, salt water taffy, more gummy worms, a canister of coffee, gooey caramel cubes, a book of Mad Libs, a couple coloring books and a box of markers.

Finley licked his lips at the goodies then showed his own stash of treats and activities: several cans of cola, two large bags of chips (sour cream with onion, and classic salt), a deck of cards, some comic books, a copy of *The Lion, The Witch and the Wardrobe* and, of course, the library book called *Ghosts, Ghouls and Goblins: Scary Short Stories.*

Leah laughed when she saw C. S. Lewis's book. "Great story. Now I wish we had some Turkish Delight."

"Did you know Mr. Lewis was actually born in Ireland? Most people think of him as British."

"No…how do you know that?"

He shrugged. "I saw it in a documentary once. Anyway, I thought it might be a good idea to start the night off with an adventure book and save the ghost stories for when we're sleepy. They'll help us stay awake."

"I don't need a story to stay awake," Leah said as she lifted the canister. "I secretly made us some coffee while Mom and Dad were at work."

He frowned. "Why is it a secret?"

"Because I never drink coffee. If they found out I made some, they'd ask why and then I'd have to explain it was for tonight. Then they'd ask why again and I'd have to tell them about us staying awake for twenty-four hours straight. Then they'd ask why again and I'd have to tell them about our summer list. Long story short, everything's a secret."

"Or you could lie."

"Finn, you know I'm a terrible liar. That's why I have to be sneaky, instead."

He laughed. "If they ever catch you leaving through your bedroom window, they'll put bars on it."

Leah laughed along. "I'll just have to keep being sneaky."

They shuffled around their snacks and blankets until they were satisfied with the arrangement.

"Shhhh," Leah said suddenly. "I think your mom's coming."

Finley threw a blanket over her head. "Hide. Don't move."

Her voice was muffled. "Hey."

"Shhhh." He sat in the tree house entryway and dangled his feet over the edge. "Hey, Mom. What's up?"

"I just wanted to say good night." She looked up at him. "Do you have everything you need for tonight?"

"Yes, I have everything."

"Did you brush your teeth? Floss?"

"Yes and no."

She gave him a look. "You'll get cavities if you don't floss."

"I know, I know. I'll do it in a bit, OK?"

"OK, Finley. I'll leave the back door unlocked; if it gets too cold out here, you can come inside."

"Thanks, Mom."

She stood there for a moment longer. "Aren't you going to come down for a good night hug?"

Finley chuckled nervously. "Oh, yeah, coming."

"Good night, dear," she said, as she hugged him. "Have a good sleep in your tree house. I love you."

He mumbled, "Love you, too. G'night, Mom."

He watched as she headed back into the house and waited until the kitchen light turned off. Only then was he confident enough to sigh in relief and climb back up the tree.

He whispered. "We're in the clear. She didn't see you."

Leah threw the blanket off her head. "Wicked, cool. What do you wanna do first?"

"I don't know about you but I'm gonna feast."

They opened all their bags of goodies and munched into the late hours of the night. Leah colored as Finley read aloud about Lucy discovering Narnia and the Pevensie children having dinner with Mr. and Mrs. Beaver. When he grew tired of reading, Leah prompted him to provide words for a couple Mad Libs. She stopped after he kept repeating the words 'fart', 'butt' and 'stinky'. It was just after one in the morning and he was getting pretty giggly. She, on the other hand, was starting to feel a little grouchy and sleepy.

"I'm gonna try some coffee," she said and poured some into the lid of the canister.

"Already? I'm not even tired," Finn said as he flopped face-first into a pillow.

The coffee was lukewarm and had been sitting in the canister for about eight hours. She hadn't tasted it before packing but figured it wouldn't be that bad. Her dad drank it with a little cream but her mom had it black. Leah decided to not add any extras and be a coffee-purist. She took a sip and immediately wanted to spit it back out. Instead, she fought the urge and awkwardly held it in her mouth, while deciding what to do.

Finn regarded her from his pillow. "How is it?"

She managed to swallow. "Blech. It needs sugar. Lots of it."

"Really? Let me try some."

She handed him the lidless canister and warily watched him take a sip. Unlike her, he spat his back into the canister.

"That. Is. Gross." He wiped his mouth with the back of his hand. "How do my parents drink this toxic stuff?"

Leah took a swig of cola and swished it in her mouth. "Diane always gets those special drinks in restaurants, the ones with tons of sugar and whipped cream. I just thought she had a sweet tooth but now I understand."

"That sounds much better. I can't drink it black."

"Well, I'm not drinking it now that you spat in it. Take these." She handed him some caramel cubes then dropped some into her own drink.

"I'm adding a couple of those peanut butter, chocolate things too. I gotta make this drinkable."

By the time their coffee tasted sweet, it had become a thick, brown sludge. Drinkable, yes, still gross, though. They finished their drinks, one grimaced swallow at a time; soon after, Finley was bouncing up and down.

"I'm bored," he complained. "Let's read a ghost story now. The caffeine made me hyper."

"All right," Leah agreed. "Do you want me to read aloud or will you?"

Finn aimed his flashlight underneath his chin, casting long, dark shadows upon his face. "Wha-ha-ha. I'll have the pleasure of reading aloud, if you please."

"Go for it."

"I do the voices better," he announced as he clawed at his own face and bulged his eyes out.

"All right."

"And I can add sound effects if you—"

Leah laughed. "Will you just read it? Come on. This is what we've been waiting for all night."

He took the book and dramatically flipped the pages to the first short story. He cleared his throat, preparing himself to change his voice for each character and read, "The Ghost of Thompson Manor."

The Ghost of Thompson Manor

Henry and his family had just moved into the neighborhood. His mother was hired as the new second grade teacher and thought a change in scenery would be good for everyone after her husband died. Henry missed his father a lot and made the mistake of mentioning this to his classmates during his first day at school. Now, a couple of the boys from his class, Jason and Chad, bullied

Henry. They called him 'Daddy's baby'. His sister, Jane, was two years younger than him and had stopped talking to anyone other than her family. She was too sad and shy to make new friends, even if her classmates were nicer than Henry's.

One day. as Henry and Jane were walking home from school, the bullies followed them and threatened to punch Henry.

"C'mon, Jason, hit the baby," Chad yelled in Henry's ear.

"Maybe he should try to hit me first." Jason laughed. "Then I can say I was only defending myself."

"Leave me alone," Henry muttered.

"Oooh, leave him alone," Chad teased. "You're hurting his feelings."

"I think his sister is going to cry." Jason laughed again. "Are you scared of us, widdle gurl?"

Henry looked down at his sister and could tell she was holding back tears. "Don't talk to her," he said.

Jason sneered. "Make me stop."

Henry could bear their bullying but he wasn't going to put up with them bullying his sister, too. He pushed Jason in the chest with all of his strength then grabbed Jane's hand. "Run."

Chad helped Jason up to his feet then they chased after the siblings. Even though Henry and Jane were smaller, their fear made them run faster than ever before. They cut through a couple lawns, over a short fence and came across a large hedge.

"Stop, stop," Henry told Jane and they hid behind the bushes.

They were breathing heavily and could hear the two bullies yelling somewhere but couldn't see them. Gradually, their breathing slowed down as the mean voices disappeared.

"Are they gone?" Jane whispered.

"I think so," Henry replied then took her hand again. "Let's go home."

They emerged from the hedge and tried to figure out which way home was. As they turned around, they realized exactly where they were... Thompson Manor.

Finley cast the flashlight over his face and added dramatically, "Dun-dun-duuuuuuuun."

Leah giggled. "Go on."

It was a three-story Victorian house with two creepy dragon statues at the base of the stairs leading to the front door. The wooden walls were as dark as the black roof and the windows seemed to suck in the sunlight instead of reflect it. The lawn was covered in scraggly weeds and the trees were twisted and full of knots.

"Whoa." Jane gasped.

"We'd better go," Henry said. "Mr. Thompson probably doesn't want us on his yard."

As they were leaving, Jane looked over her shoulder at the house. "It's beautiful, isn't it?"

Her brother glanced at her. "The house?"

"Yes."

"I think it looks kinda creepy."

The next day at school, Henry managed to completely avoid Jason and Chad. As soon as the final bell rang, he grabbed his backpack and dashed out of the classroom. He hoped to get home as fast as possible but he had to wait for Jane at the school exit. By the time she finally arrived, most of the other kids had left.

"My teacher wants me to give this note to Mom." She handed it to Henry. "She's worried because I don't speak in class."

"She doesn't know what she's talking about," Henry said and slipped the note into his sister's backpack. "Let's get outta here before Jason and Chad find us."

But just as they exited the doors, there they were.

"Missed you in class, Baby Henry," Chad jeered.

"We were worried you couldn't play today," Jason mocked.

"Leave me alone. I just want to go home," Henry said.

He tried to move past them but they blocked his way.

"No way, loser. You're hanging out with us today," Chad said.

Jason held out his fists. "Look, I even have a snack for you. I call it a knuckle sandwich. Ha."

He punched Henry in the arm and he stumbled backward.

"You're not going anywhere." Chad tried to grab him but missed.

Henry and Jane ran down the street and around the corner but this time Jason and Chad caught up to them. The bullies grabbed Henry and were just about to punch him, when they heard a bone-chilling scream. They all stopped in their tracks and looked around. Once again, the siblings realized they were in front of Thompson Manor.

"Whoa, it's the Thompson place," Chad muttered.

Henry scrambled out of the boys' grasp and stood by his sister. He asked her, "Where did that scream come from?"

She shrugged.

Jason smirked as his gaze slowly fell on Henry. "Hey, little baby. I've got an idea. You want us to leave you alone?"

Henry nodded.

Jason continued, "I'm tired of chasing you around all the time. I dare you to go into this house and wave at us from the third floor window." He pointed to the dark glass at the top peak of the house. "If you do that, we'll leave you alone for the rest of the week."

Henry shook his head defiantly. "I'm not going to trespass on someone's property just so you'll leave me alone for a week."

Chad crossed his arms. "Fine. Then we'll just have to beat you up."

"Wait." Jason pondered an idea. "How about this...If you complete my dare, we'll leave you alone for the rest of the year." Chad looked at his friend in confusion, before Jason added, "But if you don't do it...you have to wait for us after school so we can punch you. Every day, until we graduate."

"Both Jason and I get to punch you," Chad added. "That's two punches every day."

Leah pulled a blanket closer to her chest. "No way. I'd never accept that dare."

Finley looked up from the story. "But if Henry does it, he won't get bullied and it's an easy one to win."

"But they have to trespass," Leah argued. "Who knows what'll happen to the old man who lives in that house. They could give him a heart attack. They could become murderers."

"Let's just see what happens." Finley began reading again.

Henry looked at his little sister and knew what he had to do. He had to accept the dare.

"You have to leave my sister alone, too."

Jason shrugged. "Fine. You're more fun to punch, anyway."

Henry nodded. "OK...I'll do it. But Jane's staying here."

She tugged on his arm and violently shook her head. She wasn't going to let him go through with it alone. She was coming with him.

"I can't let you do this," Henry argued.

She squeezed his hand and he knew she wasn't going to give up. She was determined to come along.

"OK, we're both going." Henry held out his free hand for Jason to shake.

"One thing you should know before you go in." Jason smirked. "The place is haunted."

Chad smiled wickedly. "No one knows how Mr. Thompson died...but some say he was murdered."

"And he's waiting to get revenge on his murderer," Jason explained. "So now he haunts the house, waiting to strike." He grabbed Henry's hand and shook it hard.

"Uh-uh. No way. Don't go in there." Leah flung the blanket over her head and peeked out at Finley from a small gap.

"Will you let me read?" Finley huffed impatiently.

"Sorry."

"Don't wet your pants, Daddy's baby." Chad laughed.

"Look at them," Jason said as Henry and Jane trudged down the pathway toward the house. "Holding hands. I'm surprised they're not sucking their thumbs, too."

They laughed together.

"Five bucks says they don't even reach the second floor before running back out of the house," Chad said.

"I'll take that bet," Jason agreed.

As they walked past the dragon statues, Henry said, "If I didn't know better, I'd think those eyes were following us."

Jane's own eyes were saucers. "Were they lying about that man being murdered?"

"They were just trying to scare us," Henry replied, although he wasn't confident that was true. "Of course they were lying. But just to be safe, let's find out if anyone's home before we go in."

He knocked on the door and nervously chewed on his thumbnail as they waited for a response. There wasn't one.

"Try again, loser," Chad yelled behind them.

"Maybe the ghost will answer." Jason laughed.

Henry knocked again and this time the door opened. By itself.

"Eeeeee," Leah squealed.

"Leah, you ruined the moment," Finley protested.

She squirmed in her blanket. "I couldn't help it. It's so exciting…and I didn't ruin it. If anything, I added to it. These kinds of books require a scream now and then."

"Just don't get too loud or my parents will hear you."

Henry's voice shook as he peered through the doorway. "Hello?"

There was no reply.

He called into the house one more time, "Hello? Is anyone here?"

"Just go," Chad yelled.

Carefully, they both stepped into the house. The floor creaked and the air was thick with dust. Nothing moved or made a sound.

They ascended the spiral staircase that sat at the right of the entryway.

"Careful, this one's broken." Henry guided his sister around a step with a hole in it.

"I wonder how long it's been," Jane whispered.

"What do you mean?"

"I wonder how long it's been since someone was here," she explained. "The house seems so sad, all alone."

Henry regarded his sister for a moment and marvelled at her ability to be sympathetic toward everything. Something slammed on the first floor and they froze.

Finley stomped his foot and Leah jumped.
"Don't do that," she demanded.
He chuckled. "I couldn't resist."

"What was that?" Jane asked.

Henry struggled to come up with an explanation. Finally, he weakly said, "Probably just a window shutter banging against the house or a mouse made something fall on the floor. I'm sure it's nothing important."

Jane nodded. "Maybe we should hurry, just in case."

He made it to the top of the staircase and just as Jane was going to follow him, she heard something creaking. She paused and listened to the sound get louder. And louder. Suddenly, the floorboard underneath her broke and she fell waist-deep into the hole.

"Jane." Henry ran to her and grabbed her arms. He caught her before she could fall any further.

"I'm stuck." Jane cried. "Ow."

The sharp floorboard edges clung to her clothes and scratched her skin. She kicked her feet and held tightly to her brother's arms. Slowly, he managed to pull her to safety, far away from the deep, dark hole. They both rested on the floor, panting from exhaustion and fear.

"Thanks, Henry." She hugged him close.

"Come on, let's go." He helped his sister to her feet. "The sooner we're out of here, the better."

At the end of the hall was a door as red as blood. It was the only room on the third floor with a window facing the front lawn.

Henry led the way and twisted the door knob. The door opened silently.

"There's the window," Jane whispered.

Henry walked over and peered through the grimy glass. He saw Jason and Chad looking up at him and waved. Their mouths dropped when they saw him and they appeared to be arguing about something.

"I can't believe they did it." Jason screamed. "Why did we make this stupid bet, anyway?"

"You're the one who didn't want to chase them anymore," Chad argued. "I think chasing is half the fun."

"Shut up." Jason punched Chad in the arm.

"Hey." Chad punched back.

Jason shoved him. "Don't hit me."

"Don't push," Chad said, as he regained his balance.

"Wait." Jason held out his hands to shield his torso. "We should be taking out our anger on the baby, not each other."

"But he won the bet. We can't beat him up anymore."

"It was a stupid bet. You didn't think I meant it, did you?"

"Uh..."

"Of course we're not going to stop picking on him...and I just got a great idea." Jason wrung his hands together. "We're going to sneak into the house and grab them when they're close to the front door. They'll be so surprised, they won't even fight back. Then we'll lock them in a closet or bathroom or whatever."

Chad laughed. "That's amazing. They'll never see it coming."

"It'll be hilarious." Jason laughed with wicked glee.

Henry sighed with relief and turned away from the window. Jane was swaying to and fro in a chair, looking contentedly around the place.

"I wish I had a rocking chair in my bedroom." She smiled.

Henry smiled back at her then looked around the rest of the room. A movement caught his eye and he gasped. To his left was a mirror partially covered with a large drape. His reflection had scared him. He chuckled to himself and lifted the drape off, revealing the whole mirror. It was oval, about five feet long, with a wooden base and full of cracks. It distorted his reflection. Suddenly, ten eyes were looking back at him, with five noses and seven mouths. He grimaced at the unflattering boy staring back at him but couldn't seem to tear away his eyes. The jagged cracks appeared to be growing deeper into his skin, etching into his flesh. All at once, the reflection wasn't just a reflection. He could feel those cracks on his face, burning lines deep into his skin, as a knife carves wood. He tried to scream but his voice caught in his throat and his eyes remained fixed on the mirror as though cursed to stare at his doom. He could hear his flesh fizzling as the cracks grew deeper and the scent burned his nostrils. In agony, he tried screaming again but his voice had disappeared.

The next moment, he was lying on the floor. Jane had run at him from across the room and tackled him to the ground, tearing away his eyes from the mirror in the process.

He touched his face. It didn't even have a scratch from his tumble.

"What happened?" he asked.

"I don't know." Jane was breathing heavily. "Your face...it reminded me of broken china dolls...and it looked as though you were trying to move...but you couldn't."

"I couldn't look away." He wiped a tear from his cheek.

"Run," a soft voice said.

"What?" he asked.

"I didn't say anything," Jane replied.

"Run," the voice said again.

Henry grabbed Jane's hand. "I think we need to get out of here. Now."

They rushed out of the room. Narrowly missing the hole at the top of the steps, they ran down the stairs as fast as they could. There was a loud moan from inside the house and the steps began to shift. Henry and Jane clung to the banister to keep from falling as they watched each step morph and grow two rows of sharp spikes.

"What's happening?" Jane screamed.

"They're teeth," Henry yelled back.

The steps were now moving on their own, each resembled a mouthful of razor-sharp teeth, chomping at their feet.

"Get on," Henry demanded as he hoisted himself onto the banister.

Jane followed his lead and they slid down all the way to the first floor. They scrambled to the front door and tugged at it. It didn't budge.

"The back. Try the back door." Henry yelled.

They ran to the back but Jane couldn't open it either.

"Wait." She tugged at the deadbolt, straining against years of rust buildup.

"Together." Henry said and wrapped his hands around hers.

The bolt jerked slightly. Then some more. Again, the house moaned menacingly. Abruptly, a glass cup flew at Jane's head. She shrieked and ducked just before it hit her.

"Got it," Henry said as the lock opened. "Turn the doorknob."

Jane threw open the door and they ran out, narrowly missing a flying plate. The door slammed shut behind them and they ran halfway down the block before stopping.

Jason and Chad quietly opened the front door. Inside was brighter than they'd expected, which made sneaking around much easier.

"Let's hide behind that couch," Jason said, pointing to the living room.

Chad stifled a laugh. "This is going to be so good. I can't wait to see their faces when we catch them."

"Shhhh. You hide on the left side and I'll hide on the right."

"I wonder where they are now." Chad chuckled.

Jason lifted a hand to his ear. "Shut up. I hear footsteps."

"What about those two boys who keep picking on you?" Jane asked. "Do you think they're in trouble?"

Henry rubbed his forehead, desperately wanting to leave them behind and just go home. But one look at Jane's eyes made him realize he had to do the right thing.

"I guess we should go back and see if they're still on the front yard."

When they got there, however, no one was in sight.

Jason peered from behind the couch, looking first at the stairs then the door. No one was there.

"Where are they?" Chad whispered.

"I don't see them. I'm going to get a better view," Jason replied as he backed away from his hiding spot.

Suddenly, the couch cushions jumped five feet in the air and the couch's frame opened up as a mouth, swallowing Chad whole.

"Help," he screamed, just before the cushions rested back on the furniture, as if nothing had happened.

Jason stared in horror. He could hear muffled shouting from inside the couch but was too afraid to touch it, in case it swallowed him, too.

"Chad?" He paused for a moment, thoughts racing through his mind. "I have to get out of here," he finally told himself. "I gotta get out while I still can."

He ran to the front door but before he could reach it, a blue figure floated down from the ceiling. His head only had a few strands of hair left and his mouth was full of rotten teeth. His cheekbones and jaw stuck out harshly from his skull, making his eyes look sunken in. He hovered above Jason with a sinister expression on his face.

"How dare you enter my house," he proclaimed.

Jason's eyes became huge. "Huh?"

"You and another have entered my domain without permission. No one may roam within these walls without my approval."

"No, it wasn't me," Jason's voice cracked. "There were two other kids walking in your house. I was just leaving. I wanted—"

"Silence," the ghost demanded. "Do you know who I am?"

"M—Mister Thom—Thompson?"

"You know I'm the owner of this property yet you deem yourself worthy to enter uninvited?" The ghost's lip curled in disdain. "Where two have entered, two shall be punished."

Jason argued, "But I'm not the one that—"

"Two shall be punished." The ghost drew near to him.

"Jason and Chad probably left after they saw me in the window," Henry reasoned. "They looked angry because I won the bet."

"I take back what I said about the house being beautiful," Jane said as they stared at the building. "Someone should tear it down."

"No one will believe us if we tell them what happened. Maybe we should just keep it a secret. Otherwise, they'll think we're crazy."

"Maybe we are?"

Henry paused then said, "When we were in the house...I heard something."

"Me too. It moaned."

He shook his head. "No. I heard a voice."

"A voice?"

"It told me to run. Right after you saved me from the mirror."

"Who was it?"

"I think...I think it was Dad."

Jane looked at her brother and smiled. She took his hand and together they walked home. They'd won the bet. Henry wouldn't be bullied anymore and they were safe.

Meanwhile, back at Thompson Manor, faint screams were heard from the inside...
The End.

Finley and Leah stared at one another after the story ended.

He tried to laugh but it sounded fake. "That wasn't scary."

"Yeah," Leah scoffed. "I don't know why people make such a big deal about ghost stories."

He hesitated. "Should I read another one?"

"No," she answered quickly. "I mean...I'm not in the mood right now. Maybe later."

"Yeah, sure." He put the book down.

Leah had to go to the bathroom but didn't want to be alone now. She knew it was silly to feel scared yet the darkness around her had become ominous. Finley felt the same way but wouldn't admit it. If everyone in the story had a happy ending, he would've felt fine but the scream at the end played in his head over and over. Suddenly, something creaked outside the tree house.

"What was that?" Leah looked around.

"Probably one of the tree branches moving in the wind," he reasoned.

"But it's not very windy," she argued.

He couldn't provide a better answer so he changed the subject. "Let's play a card game. How about crazy eights?"

Grateful for something to do, Leah accepted the suggestion. Several times they heard the creak again but they ignored it and filled the silence by talking about nothing particularly interesting. It felt as though an eternity had passed.

"What time is it?" Leah asked, fidgeting uncomfortably because she still hadn't gone to the bathroom.

Finley checked his watch. "Four o'clock. I think the sun rises around five-thirty."

"I guess I drank too much coffee," Leah finally admitted. "Did I hear your mom say the backdoor to your house is unlocked?"

"Yes."

"I'll be right back."

She crawled out of the tree house and quickly climbed down the ladder, reminding herself to be sensible. The steps wouldn't turn into wooden teeth or bite her feet. Finley's house wasn't haunted but it was inhabited by his parents so she'd have to be quiet. She covered half of her flashlight with her thumb so she wouldn't shine too much light and draw attention to herself. Carefully, she crept down the hall and found the bathroom.

Meanwhile, Finley waited in the tree house. Everything sounded louder now that he was alone. The creaking noise continued and the crickets were practically screaming in his ears. He grabbed a gummy worm and chewed it nervously, trying to focus on one of his comic books.

When did nighttime become so noisy? And what's taking Leah so long? he wondered. *She's been gone for at least ten minutes by now. I hope my parents didn't catch her…or something worse.* He gazed at the backdoor but nothing stirred. *Should I go see if something's wrong? No, I'm overreacting.*

Nothing is—He jumped when a dog down the street barked at something. *Stop it.* He rebuked himself and munched on another gummy worm.

Leah peered out of the bathroom, worried the sound of the toilet flushing had woken up Finley's parents. When she saw the coast was clear, she tiptoed to the back door and carefully closed it behind her. Then she ran to the tree and scampered back up the ladder. Finley hadn't heard her cross the yard so he jumped when her head popped into sight. For a split second, they saw the fear in each other's eyes. Then they broke down and laughed at themselves.

"I didn't hear you come. You scared me so bad," Finn said, grabbing his stomach.

She pointed a finger at him. "Serves you right for stomping your foot during the story and scaring me."

Together they felt safe again. The ghost story lingered in the back of their minds until the sun rose but they passed the remaining time quickly, without any more scares. Around six-thirty, Finley snuck into the house for his own bathroom break and grabbed some breakfast on the way back, which consisted of a couple pieces of bread and fruit for each of them. Their eyes were red and half-closed, both looked pale and Finn had dark circles around his eyes, whereas the corners of Leah's mouth drooped; but they made it. After counting down the last few seconds to 8 o'clock and giving each other a victorious high five, Leah tossed her things into her bag, scuttled down the block and snuck back into her bedroom through the window. At 11 o'clock, her mother came to her room to check on her. She was surprised to see Leah still in bed.

"Usually it's Diane who sleeps so late. I suppose you're becoming more of a teenager," she said as she brushed Leah's hair from her face.

"I didn't sleep very well last night," Leah tried to explain.

"Perhaps you should go to bed early tonight." Her mom chuckled. "We don't want you to sleep during church, do we?"

Meanwhile, Finley slept in the tree house until the summer heat made it unbearable to stay any longer. With bloodshot eyes and sweat-drenched clothes, he shuffled through the house, avoiding his parents' questioning gazes. After emerging from his cold shower, his mom asked if he had a good sleep in the tree house.

"Nah," he replied. "I don't think I'll do it again anytime soon."

He thought he saw his parents give one another a knowing glance but it was so quick, he may have misinterpreted it.

Leah and Finn's List for an Awesome Summer

~~1. Eat a whole gallon of ice cream (each)~~

2. Build a throne

3. Take a dance class

~~4. Hunt crabs at night, at the beach~~

5. Sneak into an R rated movie at the theater

6. Drive a car

7. Discover a new world

~~8. Stay awake for 24 hours straight~~

9. Find buried treasure

~~10. Attempt a world record~~

11

"I slept practically all Saturday," Finley said when a commercial appeared on the TV.

"I slept for a couple hours then Mom woke me up," Leah commented. "I could barely keep my eyes open for the rest of the day. I think I went to bed at seven. Hey, you want something to drink?" She meandered to the kitchen.

"Do you have apple juice?"

"Yep." She came back with two full cups and handed him one.

He continued, "Out of everything we've done this summer, I think staying awake all night had the worst aftereffects."

"I almost fainted. And you puked from the ice cream," Leah reminded.

"Yeah but I only felt sick for a couple hours…"

"And now you hate anything that's mint chocolate chip flavoured."

"…OK, you're right. That one was the worst."

"Hey, I was thinking about what we should do next." Leah sat straighter on the couch. "Diane said she's going to the beach with her friends tomorrow. Maybe we should go with and look for buried treasure."

"What, we're pirates now?"

"Hardy-har-har," she replied sarcastically. "Do you have any better suggestions?"

"That's actually not a bad idea," Finn pondered. "Things are always washing onto shore. We could find something in the sand or the water. Besides, we're not little kids anymore… We know we'll never actually find gold coins. It could be a good compromise."

She scoffed. "What do you mean it's a compromise?"

"Nothing. When we added 'find buried treasure' to the list, I just assumed we'd be digging in a forest or searching in a cave."

"With that logic we should just root around in our grandparents' attics and find a map with an 'X' on it."

"That's what makes your idea good," he explained, trying to smooth over the situation. "It's so practical. Oh, the show's back on."

The next day Leah convinced her sister to bring them along.

"Why do you guys have shovels?" Diane asked as they got in the car.

Leah looked to Finley for help. Her mind was drawing a blank for a reasonable excuse and she knew she couldn't get away with a lie.

Finley replied nonchalantly, "We're going to bury a body."

Diane huffed. "Never mind, don't tell me. And when we get to the beach, please remember to not bother me while I'm with my friends."

"Why don't you want us around?" Finley asked innocently.

"You know why," Diane said, her eyes focused on the road.

Leah smirked at Finley. "She doesn't want us to bother her when there are boys around."

He gasped mockingly. "Diane, is that true? There are boys at the beach?"

"Why don't you zip it?" Diane glanced back at them. "I can always turn around and leave you at home."

"Zip it?" Leah giggled.

"Potty language." Finley burst out laughing.

Diane pulled over on the side of the road and looked back at them. "I'm serious. One more word and I'm turning around. Got it?"

They stopped laughing and nodded silently.

"Good."

She turned back onto the highway.

"We're pretty good at making teenagers angry at us while they're driving," Finley whispered to Leah.

She giggled in response and Diane's eyes shot daggers at them from the rear-view mirror.

"No noise at all," she said. "I'm serious."

Leah stifled her laughter as Finley made goofy faces for the rest of the trip. After finding a parking spot, Diane handed Leah a fistful of cash.

"This is for lunch so don't lose it," she warned.

Leah stuffed it into her bag. "Thanks."

Diane led them to the beach. "Did you put on sunscreen already?"

Leah rolled her eyes. "Yes. We're fine."

"Meet you back at the car at four o'clock. Mom wants us home in time to help prepare supper tonight. She's got a meeting and Dad's picking her up afterward so they'll both be home a little late. Do you have your watch with you?"

"Yes, I got it," Leah whined. "You don't have to babysit me all the time. I have my sunscreen, my watch, my water bottle…"

Diane opened the car trunk and replied snidely, "Don't forget your shovels."

Leah muttered something unflattering about her sister as she brought them out and slammed the trunk lid closed.

"Have fun with your friends." Finley waved, resembling a proud father. "Wait an hour after you eat before you go swimming. And don't talk to strangers."

Diane lifted an eyebrow at him before sauntering off.

He smiled at Leah and teased, "I'm gonna miss her."

She punched his arm jokingly. "You can keep her."

"Ow. Forget this nonsense, let's find some pirate treasure. It's the best kind, you know."

"I want to start digging in the sand. When it starts to get hot, we can look in the water. What do you think?"

He saluted. "Aye, aye, captain."

They found a tree growing on the grassy strip of land that separated the parking lot from the beach. They dragged their stuff underneath it then looked around at the empty beach.

"Wow," Finley remarked. "It's so quiet."

Leah speculated, "I guess there aren't many people here because it's a Wednesday. The beach is always busy on the weekend." She grabbed a shovel. "Where should we start digging?"

"Pick a spot, any spot."

"I say we dig close to the water's edge."

Making his voice gravely, Finley asked, "Might there be sea monsters in yonder water?"

Leah tried to hide her smile. "Are you going to do that all day? You'll lose your voice."

He quickly composed himself. "All right, I'm done. Let's dig."

The water cooled their feet as they scooped away the sand. Unfortunately, the waves kept depositing sand back into their holes so they moved further onto shore.

"Ooh, look at this, Finn." Leah plucked a white, spiralled shell from her shovel.

"I like it. Where was it?"

"I dug it up over here," she said, pointing to her hole in the sand.

He picked up a smooth stone and tried skipping it across the water.

"I don't think that works unless the water is still," Leah commented.

"Oh, OK. So this isn't right, either?" He took a bigger rock and smashed it into the water, splashing both of them in the process.

She wiped her face. "Hey."

He thrashed in the water, intentionally splashing her more. "This is way more fun than digging."

Leah ran back to their stuff on the beach. At first Finley thought he had upset her but then he saw she was only placing her shell in her bag for safekeeping. When she ran back, she playfully rammed into him and they both fell into the water.

She sputtered, "You're right. That is fun."

They spent the rest of the morning simply having fun. They swam deeper into the water, tagged the other before running away and scared each other by hiding underwater and then suddenly emerging. They totally forgot about completing their summer list and just enjoyed being kids.

Around twelve-thirty they emerged from the water, beaming and breathless.

"I'm starving," Finley said, dragging both of their shovels behind him. "Let's get something to eat."

Leah grabbed their lunch money. "I'm more thirsty than anything else."

He dropped the shovels with the rest of their stuff before shuffling to the nearest concession stand. They purchased their meal then contentedly consumed their hot dogs and chocolate milk in the shade of a nearby tree.

"This is so good." Leah licked ketchup from her fingers. "I'm gonna get another one. You want one?"

"Mmm-hmm." Finley chewed the last of his bun.

"I'll be right back."

She rushed back to the stand and patiently waited her turn in line. A boy about her age was standing in front and turned around when he noticed her.

"Hey, Leah." He flashed a charming grin.

She was momentarily caught off guard. "Hey, Grant. I didn't know you were here today." She tried not to blush when she looked into his eyes. *They're gorgeous,* she thought.

"Nice day to be at the beach, isn't it?"

She nodded. "Yeah, it is. What are you up to today?"

He pointed to a man standing beside a nearby truck. "Dad and I are going hiking and thought we'd grab some food before taking off."

"Oh, do you guys go hiking a lot?"

He chuckled. "No, only when he's on vacation."

"Next," the cashier said.

"Oh, sorry." He stepped up to the counter and ordered two hot dogs.

He looked back at Leah. "I can't get enough of these dogs."

"They're the best around." She giggled nervously.

"Thanks." He grabbed his food. "See you around, Leah."

"Bye." With butterflies in her stomach, she watched him leave.

"What can I get you?" the cashier asked.

She stared at him, her mind suddenly blank. "Uh…water, please. No. Actually, two hot dogs, please."

"Why are you smiling?" Finn asked when she returned.

"No reason." She bit her lip and handed him a hot dog. "It's just a good day."

After they finished eating, they decided to walk further up the beach where the sand was rockier. This time, Leah brought along her bag in case they found anything else worth keeping and Finn carried the shovels.

"Ouch, the sand here hurts my bare feet." Leah winced.

"But it's more interesting." Finley picked up a smooth rock. "Look, it's broken in half and the center is orange."

She inspected it. "Wow, that's so cool."

He stuck it into his pocket and they looked around some more.

"What's that sparkling thing?" Leah walked over and picked up the item. "Finley, come here."

He scurried over and examined the object. It was a smooth, blue piece of glass.

"It's practically identical to a jewel," he marvelled. "I didn't know there was beach glass here."

"That's what this is?"

"Yeah, I saw it in a movie once. Glass bottles, or whatever, break into pieces and smooth out over time from the water and sunlight. Pretty cool."

She watched the sun glint off the piece in her hand. "I wonder if there's any more. I've never been to this part of the beach before."

Finley positioned himself so the sun was out of his eyes. "I guess it's kinda far from everything else. People probably don't come by here too often—Hey, there's something."

"Where?"

He picked up another piece, this one was white and triangular. "It's in the shape of a heart."

"This really feels as though we're finding buried treasure." Leah grinned.

They scoured the ground for the next half an hour then raked their shovels over the sand to reveal more underneath. After another two hours, their necks and shoulders ached from digging and looking down for so long. Their feet were also sore from the rough terrain but they were in good spirits. They had a beautiful collection of about fifteen pieces each. Most of them were amber or white but they'd found a few that were green, blue and yellow. In addition, they'd found several interesting stones and shells to keep. By the end of the day, Leah's bag and Finn's pockets were heavy.

He tightened the drawstring of his swim trunks to keep them up. "Maybe we should head back to the main beach. It must be getting close to four o'clock."

Leah pulled her watch out of her bag. "You're right. I'm surprised we found so much cool stuff. I wish we'd found this place sooner."

"We can always come back," Finley said. "My pockets are pretty full anyway."

"I should bring some of this stuff to the cabin and make it into jewellery."

Finley eyed her neck. "Whoa, the back of your neck is sunburned."

She instinctively touched her skin. It was prickly. "Oh no. I should have put on more sunscreen after lunch." She pointed to Finn. "And you have a sunburn on your back. I think you missed a spot with the sunscreen."

He twisted his body, trying to look at his back. "I don't see anything."

"Trust me, it's there."

They meandered back to the car just before Diane arrived. She looked them up and down.

"Did you guys put on *any* sunscreen?" she asked.

Leah grimaced. "Do we look that bad?"

"You don't," Diane replied, "but he does."

Finley raised his arms. "…Oops?"

"Glad it's you and not me." Diane unlocked the car doors. "Get in."

As soon as their bare skin touched the hot seats in the car, Leah and Finley cried out in pain.

"I told you guys to wear sunscreen." Diane chuckled.

"Zip it," Leah and Finley yelled in unison.

Leah and Finn's List for an Awesome Summer

1. ~~Eat a whole gallon of ice cream (each)~~

2. Build a throne

3. Take a dance class

4. ~~Hunt crabs at night, at the beach~~

5. Sneak into an R rated movie at the theater

6. Drive a car

7. Discover a new world

8. ~~Stay awake for 24 hours straight~~

9. ~~Find buried treasure~~

10. ~~Attempt a world record~~

12

It had been four days since they were at the beach and both of their sunburns had faded. Thankfully, they hadn't been bad enough for their skin to peel but for the past several days Leah and Finley hadn't done much at home except rest their sore muscles and put ice on their flaming skin.

"I want to build the throne before you leave," he mentioned as they walked back from the convenience store.

Leah had been craving a cherry slushie all weekend and was happily sipping away. "Your tongue is blue."

"Well, it's called blue raspberry," he teased.

She rolled her eyes. "Whatever. Anyway, why do you want to build it before I go to the cabin?"

"I don't know how long it'll take to build. We might not have enough time to finish it after you come back."

She shrugged. "We'll still have two weeks."

"But after we build it, we might want to add some wood carvings or paint it or something. The other things on our summer list are easier to complete in a day or two. We can cram them into the last two weeks, if we need."

"That reminds me, July ends next week."

"Yeah? So?"

"Don't you remember? The theater always shows horror movies during the last week. On Friday we should check the newspaper to see if any are R-rated."

Finley slurped then quickly winced. "Ah. Brain freeze."

"How are we going to build a throne anyway? I mean, where do we start? And where are we going to build it?"

He rubbed his forehead. "I was thinking about that earlier. There's some extra wood from the tree house in my garage. Dad's got a bunch of tools we can use, too; but I'll have to ask his permission first."

She suggested, "Everything's already at your place. Let's just build it in your backyard. Unlike all the other things we've done, I don't think we can keep this a secret."

He agreed, "No…but it's not as though we're doing anything bad, either."

"Bad?"

"Yeah. Eating way too much ice cream or sneaking to the beach at night, for instance. We won't get in trouble for doing it."

Leah sucked the last bit of slushie from her cup. "That's true."

"Let's head over to my place and see how much wood we have to work with. Then we can ask Dad if we're allowed to use his stuff."

"Maybe he could help us with some of it," she proposed.

"No," Finley said, adamantly. "That wasn't the goal. The point is to do it ourselves."

"But what if we don't know how to do something?"

He shrugged. "We'll figure it out."

"What if we do a terrible job?"

"It can't be that hard…It's a big chair."

Leah persisted. "What if it's so bad we can't even sit in it?"

"It won't be."

"But what if it is?"

"Fine," he relented. "If we can't sit in it, we can ask for help."

"Thanks."

"But it won't be that bad," he insisted. "We have everything we need to do a great job."

"Except knowledge and experience," she mumbled.

"Come on, Leah. I let you put 'take a dance class' on our list. Now you have to help me with my thing."

"All right," she gave in, as they walked up the driveway. "Hey, this project was your idea. You should draw a picture of how you want it to look."

"I don't think we need that," he replied. "A throne is just a chair but bigger."

"May I remind you of our Alka Seltzer rocket experiment?"

"Would you quit bringing that up?" he huffed. "I made one mistake and you won't let me forget it."

"OK, OK, I'm sorry. I won't bring it up again."

"Really?"

She nodded sincerely. "Really."

"Thanks." He opened the garage door and showed her the pile of scrap wood in the corner.

"Now what?" Leah asked.

"Hey guys." Mr. Davidson peeked inside. "What are you doing?"

"Hi, Dad."

"You have good timing, Mr. Davidson." Leah smiled. "We were just going to look for you."

He grinned back. "Oh? Can I help you with anything?"

"Dad, we were wondering if we could use this scrap wood for a project?"

"Sure, go for it. What's your project?"

Finley replied excitedly, "We're going to make a throne."

"A throne? I haven't seen many of those in my lifetime." His dad chuckled. "You're both going to work on it?"

"Yep," Leah confirmed. "But my parents don't have the tools we need. Can we borrow yours?"

"As long as you know how to operate them safely, you're welcome to use them. The drill and hammers are fine but if you're hoping to use the table saw, I want either Finley's mother or myself to monitor the situation."

Leah gave him a 'thumbs up'. "You got it."

"Actually, Dad, could we use the hand saw instead?"

"Ah." His father shoved his hands in his pockets. "You want to make it all by hand, is that it?"

Finn nodded.

"Sure, if you have the patience and time, I say go for it; but make sure to wear the cut-proof gloves I keep over here." He picked up a pair of gloves from the sawhorse. "And wear safety goggles, too. I want you kids safe. Understand?"

"Yes," Finley and Leah replied in unison.

"Great. So, what's your design? Do you have any plans drawn up or need help figuring out the measurements you need?"

Leah regarded Finn. "Not yet…"

"We're going to play it by ear," he explained. "We'll get a general idea of the size and work from that."

"OK… Well, if you need any help or need something explained, just ask." Mr. Davidson motioned to the tree house and winked. "I have some experience with construction."

"Thanks," Leah said.

"Yeah, thanks, Dad."

Mr. Davidson started walking back to the house then remembered why he'd gone outside. "Oh, I almost forgot to mention supper will be ready in about half an hour, Finley. Are you joining us, Leah?"

"No, but thanks, Mr. Davidson."

"All right, have fun, kids."

"Let's move the wood to the backyard and get a good look at everything," Finn suggested.

They agreed then sorted the wood into smaller piles, depending on their length.

"What now?" Leah asked, wiping some sawdust from her arm.

"I think we should use the longest pieces of wood for the backrest. Then we can add the chair's seat and armrests onto those pieces."

"What about the legs?"

"Hmm… I forgot about those. Maybe we should make those first and put them on a seat?"

She shrugged. "You're the boss."

"No, wait. We should cut these four pieces of wood first," he instructed. "Then they'll be ready for the backrest; maybe we can use whatever we cut off for something else."

"OK."

He counted on his fingers. "We'll need a measuring tape, a pencil to mark where to cut the wood, the sawhorse, a handsaw, gloves and eyeglasses."

"Finley, supper's ready," his mom called out the kitchen window.

"OK, Mom."

"I better go," Leah said.

He asked, "Do you want to keep working on it after supper?"

A large gray cloud moved over the sun, casting dark shadows over the lawn.

She answered, "I think that cloud's trying to warn us of a storm tonight."

He looked up. "I don't remember hearing the weatherman say anything about rain."

She shrugged. "Before I go, do you want help moving the wood back into the garage?"

"Nah. After I eat, I'll probably have time to cut a couple pieces."

"I'll see you tomorrow then. Bye." She waved at his parents through the kitchen window as she headed home.

Unfortunately, his plans weren't fulfilled. After supper, he only had enough time to measure and mark the longest pieces of wood to the same length before the first few drops of rain splashed on the grass.

"No, wait," he muttered to the sky and grabbed a few pieces of lumber.

He'd underestimated how heavy and awkward transporting the pile by himself would be. The rain quickly became a downpour and he regretted not taking Leah up on her earlier offer.

"How about a hand?" His dad emerged from behind the garage and grabbed onto one side of a board.

Finley grabbed the other side and they quickly moved it to shelter.

"Thank you, Dad," Finley said after they got back in the house.

Mr. Davidson dried his face with a hand towel from the bathroom. "You're welcome. If I'd realized what you were doing outside, I would've helped out sooner." He tossed the towel to his son and laughed. "You and a half-drowned rat could win a twin look-alike contest."

Finley laughed along. "Shucks. I think my style is more like a dog in the bathtub."

13

Leah called Finley the next morning. "What time do you want to start working?"

"I just put the wood on the driveway," he explained. "Dad said they need to dry before we can use them. Thankfully, it's supposed to be sunny all day. I double checked."

"Did they get rained on yesterday?"

"Yeah, I was too slow bringing them back into the garage."

"Oops."

"It's my fault. I'll check them later this afternoon and give you a call if they're ready."

"Okie-dokie. If I'm not around, just leave a message on our answering machine."

Leah hung up and tapped her fingers on the table. *What should I do today? Diane's still sleeping and Mom and Dad are at work. Maybe I should read the newspaper? Or have some breakfast. A fruit smoothie would be good. Or pancakes.* She checked the fridge. *Nope, we don't have enough eggs.* She settled for a bowl of puffed rice and read the comic section of the paper. When Leah finished, she rinsed out her bowl and put it in the dishwasher then listlessly wandered around. After finding the buried treasure, she'd been so glad to do nothing for a couple days and recuperate. Now though, she was bored. She wanted to do something. *Most of the stuff on TV at this hour is for little kids or boring talk shows and I don't want to re-watch a movie.* Her fingers were clacking against the tabletop again. *I could paint my nails… Yes and I'll listen to my Adventures in Odyssey album. I'm getting a little old to still be listening to them but so what? No one can tease me if they don't know. Besides, I still like them.*

She ran to the bathroom to grab all her nail polish bottles then to her room to get her cassette player and tapes. She settled herself at the foot of her bed and painted slowly to cover every last millimeter of her nails. By the time she finished listening to the second episode, each one was a different bright color; after four episodes, her toenails were clipped and painted to match her fingers. She sighed in satisfaction. *Now what?* She cleaned up her mess and sauntered back to the kitchen, bored yet again. *It's kinda early for lunch… Ooh, I should make cookies for dessert.*

Grabbing a recipe book, she flipped to her favorite chocolate chip cookie recipe.

"It's too quiet when it's just me in here," she muttered aloud and switched on the radio.

A *Newsboys* song was playing and she sang along as she poured, cracked and mixed all the ingredients together. The air was filled with the scent of sweet vanilla and chocolate by the time Diane entered the room.

She yawned and looked around. "What's going on?"

"It's cookie time." Leah grinned.

"Why are you making cookies? Are we having company over?"

She took the last cookie pan out of the oven. "No. I was bored and wanted to have some after lunch."

"After lunch? Don't you mean have them for lunch?" Diane teased and bit into one that had been cooling on the counter.

"No," Leah reiterated. "After."

"Whatever." Diane munched again.

The radio announcer interrupted them. "Next is a song from Geoff Moore and the Distance."

"Hmm," Diane considered. "I like it. It's more rock and roll than most things on this radio station."

Leah agreed, "Yeah, I like the guitar."

Diane wiped her hands on her pants and sat down at the table while Leah had a ham and cheese sandwich and cookie for lunch.

"You're not going to eat anything other than cookies?" Leah asked her sister.

"I'm craving coffee. And I'm bored. There's nothing to do around here when all my friends are busy."

"I hope we're not gonna be super bored at the cabin," Leah said, a little worried.

"There are hiking trails," Diane explained. "And last time there were board games we could play. You don't remember?"

Leah shook her head. The last time she was at the cabin, she'd been five. Diane was seven.

"I remember staying up late, seeing a big fire and the quietness of outdoors."

Diane smiled. "That's right, I forgot about the fire. There had been a thunderstorm earlier that summer and a bunch of tree branches broke. After everything was cleaned up, we had a huge bonfire."

"Maybe we can do it again?"

"I dunno. I think Dad just wants to relax with no big parties or yard work."

Leah said softly, "He still looks tired every day."

"He's still at work every day," Diane defended. "Of course he's exhausted."

"I guess."

She saw sympathy in Leah's eyes and softened her voice. "Let's get out of here."

"What?"

"Let's go do something. I still want coffee. You can get a milkshake or soda?"

Leah nodded. "OK."

They rode their bikes several blocks until they reached a little diner.

"I don't think I've been here before," Leah said, as she locked up her bike.

"This is where a bunch of high school kids hang out. It's so small; I think most people overlook it."

"And you're bringing me here?"

"You're practically in high school. Consider this an initiation."

Leah smiled. "Thanks."

Diane shrugged and entered the cafe. "Whatever. You could also consider this a test. If you embarrass me, you're banned from this place until I graduate. Got it?"

Leah ignored her command as they sat at a table by the window. "So, is this where you go after school?"

"Sometimes; or before a school dance."

Leah thought back to the movies and TV shows she'd watched about high school. She whispered, "Do you come here after you tell Mom and Dad you're going to the library to study? Or you say you're helping someone with an after-school project but you're actually hanging out with your friends here?"

"Nah, they'd kill me if they found out I lied to them."

Leah smiled. *Huh. Believe it or not, I have something in common with Diane.*

A waitress came up to their table. "What can I get you ladies today?"

"Coffee, three sugar, two cream," Diane ordered.

Leah quickly studied the plastic menu on the table. "Can I have a chocolate milkshake?"

The waitress scribbled on her notepad. "You bet. Anything else?"

"Nope," Diane answered.

"I'll be back with your order shortly."

Leah looked out the window and watched the people walk by. She absentmindedly tapped her fingers on the table.

"Nice nails," Diane mentioned.

"Thanks."

"So…what have you been up to lately?"

Leah stopped tapping. "What?"

"Well, you're not always at home so you must be busy with something."

"Oh, that's nothing. I'm just hanging out with Finley."

"I'm surprised you guys are still friends," Diane said casually as she peered out the window.

"What do you mean?"

She shrugged. "Nothing. I lost most of my friends in seventh and eighth grade. People change a lot during those years, that's all."

"Finn's a good friend," Leah defended.

"He's a pain in the butt sometimes but…yeah, he's a good one."

"You don't sound very convinced." Leah crossed her arms.

Diane turned to look at her. "I was just thinking lots of boys and girls who are friends either start dating each other or stop hanging out."

"Well, we're not dating."

"I know. You two got past that awkward stage where rumors fly around and sometimes friendships fall apart. That's something a lot of people don't do."

"OK…"

Diane exhaled sharply. "Look, I'm trying to give you a compliment. You guys made it to the other side of middle grade. It's impressive."

"Thanks…?"

"I mean, high school's hard. It helps having a friend to get through it."

Leah frowned in confusion. "I have other friends too, you know. Joy and Dawn and Lauren—"

"I know; but you and Finley have been friends forever. He's your best friend, right?"

"Yeah."

"Exactly. That's what I'm saying."

Leah stared at her, even more confused.

"You have a best friend by your side as you start high school. You're luckier than a lot of kids."

"Didn't you have a best friend when you started?"

The waitress came and put their drinks in front of them. "If you need anything else, I'll be at the counter," she said then walked away.

Diane sipped her coffee. "I had friends but you and Finley are a tighter pair. It took me a little longer to find good ones. You've already got a good one."

"True." Leah smiled and sipped her milkshake. "Mmm, this is delicious."

"Yeah, they have the best milkshakes here."

They gazed out the window as they sipped their drinks.

Quietly, Leah remarked, "I remember one day you came home from school, crying. I asked what was wrong but you screamed at me and slammed your bedroom door in my face. I mean, you really, really screamed."

Diane's eyes didn't leave the window. "Yeah, I remember. That was a bad day."

"I'd never seen you so upset before."

"Hmm… Well, girls can be vicious. Let's leave it at that."

"Diane, you used to tell me everything…"

She huffed. "I know; but there are some things you can't fully understand unless you've experienced it."

Leah huffed in return. "How do you know that? You don't know about everything I've done or been through. You're not the only one who can keep a secret."

Their eyes met and Diane asked, "You have a secret?"

"I have lots."

"Are any of them bad? Are you covering for someone or need help—"

Leah's impatience crept into her voice. "No, nothing even close to that. I know when a secret is bad and I need to tell someone. I just meant personal stuff."

Diane regarded her for a quiet moment. "When did you start getting so mature?"

"I dunno."

"It's so weird; you're starting high school in the fall. You look so young. I don't remember ever looking as young as you."

"Well, you did once," Leah said matter-of-factly.

"Not when I started high school," Diane argued. "You look as though you still need a babysitter."

"No, I don't."

Diane chuckled.

"What's so funny?" Leah asked.

She replied, "I was just thinking about my first week of high school. My friends and I wanted the older kids to think we were the same age as them so we brought a ton of makeup to school and during lunch we tried to copy the ads we saw in magazines. We looked so bad." She laughed. "You remember Megan?"

"The blond one? Yeah."

Diane rubbed her face out of embarrassment. "OK, well, she used her own foundation on me and it made me look so pale, one of my teachers sent me to the nurse's office in the afternoon."

"You're kidding." Leah laughed.

"No. I just played along and pretended I was nauseous. I went home early and hid the nurse's note from Mom and Dad. They never found out."

"Are you serious? You never told them?"

The waitress came to drop off their bill and winked at Leah, as she walked away. Evidently, she'd enjoyed hearing their laughter from the cash register.

"No way." Diane shook her head. "Then I'd have to explain everything to them and it was humiliating. I must have looked so gross with that pale, gunky makeup on me. The blue eye shadow, however, was amazing."

"I can't believe you didn't get caught."

"I've gotten away with a few things," Diane smirked, "but I'm not telling you about some of them until you're older."

"What? No, you can trust me. You just admitted I'm mature. Tell me now," Leah begged.

"Not a chance. I'm not putting those ideas

into your head. If you get caught, I'll totally get blamed for it."

"I won't get caught."

Diane shook her head vehemently. "No way. C'mon, if you're done with your milkshake, I think we should go."

During the whole ride home, Leah wondered what kind of secrets her sister was hiding. *What else has Diane gotten away with? Maybe she'd tell me if I told her about Finn's and my summer list… No, I can't do that to him. We agreed we wouldn't tell anyone. I wonder if Diane ever told anyone what she went through in junior high. What was so hard for her? Why was she crying?*

"Hey," Diane said, as she opened their front door. "Don't tell anyone about the diner, OK? It's kind of considered…I dunno, exclusive. You only know about it because you caught me in a moment of weakness. I needed coffee."

"Can I tell Finley?"

Diane sighed in exaggerated frustration. "Fine, but no one else."

Leah smiled. "You can trust me." She grabbed one of her freshly baked cookies and listened to the message Finley left on the telephone.

"I flipped the boards so the sun can soak through but I think they'll have to sit out all night to fully dry. We can start working tomorrow. Come around ten? That way we can sleep in," he explained.

14

"Hi, Leah," Finley said as she approached his driveway.

"Hey. How's it going?" she asked.

"Good. The wood's all dry and we can get to work."

"Great. Where do you want to start?"

He pointed to four long boards. "I already marked these so we can cut them to be the same length. I think we should do that first."

"All right," Leah said. "Well, this project means a lot more to you than me so I'll just follow your lead."

"Here you go," he said, handing her a pair of safety goggles and slipped on a pair of his own. "Do you want to wear these, too?" Finn handed her a pair of his father's work gloves. "Then you won't get splinters."

"Thanks." She put them on and asked, "What about you?"

"I'll wear Dad's cut-proof gloves when I'm sawing. Other than that, I'll be fine. His gloves are a little big on me; it's hard to grip stuff."

"Do you want to saw first? We can switch when you get tired."

He shrugged. "I could probably cut every piece we need without getting tired."

"OK, but leave me at least one piece to saw through. I've never done it before but it seems kinda cool."

"Let's do this."

They took a large beam of wood to the sawhorse and positioned it lengthwise on top. Leah held onto the wood at the center of the table as Finley started cutting it with a handsaw. The wood slipped from her grasp.

"Wait." She repositioned it and applied more pressure. "Now I'm ready."

Finley started again but the wood slipped again.

"I can't get a good grip," Leah said as she tried putting her body weight onto the wood. "OK, go again."

"I'll try cutting the wood with one hand and using the other to hold it steady," he suggested.

He managed to saw a half inch groove into the beam before it moved again.

"Sorry." Leah released the board. "It's hard to keep it still. Do you have anything else that can keep it steady?"

He shook his head. "I don't think so. Dad must do something differently than we're doing. He's used the sawhorse many times by himself."

"Can we put the wood on the grass?" Leah inquired. "Then I can sit on it while you cut."

"We may as well try."

Finley grabbed the saw with both hands as Leah sat on the board. They were much more successful with this tactic and he managed to cut through three of the planks before his arms felt to be jelly.

"This saw must be dull," he complained. "It's taking forever to cut through all of this."

Leah could tell he was making excuses for already being tired. She kept her snide comment to herself and instead asked, "Really? Let me try now."

"Sure," he said as they traded gloves.

It took her a few tries to grab the wood with the saw's teeth but once she got a groove in the wood she had no further troubles.

"That was more fun than I thought it'd be." She beamed at her achievement.

"I was thinking about it yesterday," Finley said as he lined up the four beams together. "If we take another piece of wood and nail it across the top of these then nailed another at the bottom, it'll become one big sheet of wood."

"This will be the backrest?"

"Yes."

Leah grabbed two smaller pieces of wood and laid them down according to his suggestion.

"How are we going to attach it to a seat?"

"We'll nail it in from the back."

She shrugged. "If you say so."

"I can see it in my head but I can't explain it very well. You'll see when we get there."

"Which one's better? Nails or screws for the backrest?"

Finley reached into his Dad's toolbox and grabbed two hammers. "We have two of these so we can work at the same time. It'll be faster." He handed her one and they shared a small bucket of nails.

"I hope I don't hit my thumb," Leah said , in a worried tone.

She held the nail in place with one hand and readied the hammer in the other. Carefully, she tapped the nail until it was far enough into the wood to stand on its own. Then she let go and hammered harder. Finley, on the other hand, hammered hard right away. Although his aim was accurate, he hit both the nail and his thumb at the same time. He gasped in pain and inspected his finger.

"Are you OK?" Leah asked.

"Fine," he muttered and tried again, this time more carefully.

They finished the board on top, which sat slightly crooked but held firm. They hammered another board along the bottom then took a step back and inspected their work.

"Looks good," Finley proclaimed. "Now let's get some wood for the throne's legs and seat."

"How do you want the seat to look?" Leah asked.

"This." He pointed to their rectangular handiwork. "A circular seat would be way too hard to make."

"We could make it into a hexagon," she suggested.

"True…" He pondered the idea. "That would make it look more interesting. OK, let's try it."

They gathered several smaller pieces of wood together, arranging them into a square.

"If we nail this together, the same way we did with the backrest…," Finley processed the idea aloud, "then we can cut off the corners of our square to make a hexagon seat."

They agreed on the plan and nailed everything together.

"This board isn't as straight as the others. There's a gap here." Leah pointed at the grass poking through two adjacent planks of wood.

He waved off the problem. "I don't think it matters. When we're done, we can put pillows on it or something. Then it'll be comfy too."

"We could wedge some of these big splinters into the hole," Leah suggested. "Or add another board across it. Maybe it'll hold more weight then."

"Why would it need to hold more weight?"

"Right now, we don't even know if it can hold our weight. What if it breaks when we're sitting on it? We'll get splinters in our butts."

Finley laughed at the imagined scenario. "I guess you're right. Better safe than sorry."

They added one more plank of wood so that four horizontal boards were nailed to three vertical ones.

Leah rubbed her neck. "What's the time, Finn? I'm getting hungry."

"One second." He ran to the kitchen window and peered through. "Wow, it's already one twenty-five."

"Time flies when you're havin' fun." She smiled. "Wanna come over to my house for lunch? I made cookies yesterday."

"All right."

They ripped off their gloves and tossed them toward the toolbox before leaving.

"This is actually going faster than I thought," she remarked. "At first, I expected this would take us all week to finish; but, at this rate, we could be done by the end of the day."

They enjoyed leftover lasagne and cookies for lunch then headed back to work. They were thankful for the fluffy white clouds, which had accumulated above. They provided some shade during the heat of the day. Nevertheless, this time they were both careful to not overextend themselves in the heat and stayed well hydrated.

"Thanks." Leah mentioned as Finley handed her a water bottle, "I never want to get heat exhaustion again. It wasn't fun."

"It doesn't feel as hot today," he added.

They stared down at their makeshift throne seat, contemplating how to cut it.

Finn spoke first. "I got it. Step one, we find the center of our square and stick a pin in it. Step two, we attach a piece of string to the pin on one end and a pencil on the other. Step three, when we stretch the pencil out, it'll draw a circle and give us the measurements we need to cut off the corners. It'll make each side of our hexagon have an equal length."

"That's a very interesting idea, Finn."

He grinned. "I know. I saw someone else do it on a TV game show."

Leah added another idea, "We can also cut the corners of the backrest so it matches the seat. It'll make the throne look more uniform."

"Wicked, cool idea."

The circle they drew on the seat wasn't quite centred but it was enough to cut the hexagon without too much trouble. The hardest part was sawing through two planks of wood at the same time while avoiding the nails. After they finished, they were left with a half-hexagon, half-oval shape. Finley said the skewed shape made it more interesting as he gleefully rounded off the top of the backrest. He and Leah were exhausted and had jelly-arms by the time they were done.

"I need a break." Leah wiped the sweat from her forehead, unknowingly leaving behind a few pieces of sawdust in the process.

"Same here." Finley guzzled his water. "It must be almost 5 o'clock, by now."

"It took us four hours to cut all of this?"

"After planning and measuring everything, yeah. I'd estimate we were sawing for about three hours."

She winced. "No wonder my arms feel so heavy."

He suggested the next step of their plan. "If we nail the seat and backrest together, we can lay it down when we put on the legs."

"Finn, I'm so tired, I don't even want to think about what we're going to do next. Let's stop for the day."

"You're right, we should stop," he agreed. "Hey, if you need any encouragement, we've done the hardest part of the work."

Leah groaned and lay down on the grass. Sometimes she thought Finley's enthusiasm was too much. Now was one of those times.

"We can nail the seat to the backrest here," he chattered to himself. "Where did those extra pieces of wood go? Oh, here they are. So if I want the throne to be this high, I'll need to cut the leg pieces about here…and attach them here."

"I think I should go home now," Leah said. "You know, so I can clean up before supper."

"Oh, yeah, sure thing. Bye, Leah. See you tomorrow."

She slowly got to her feet and shuffled home, thinking of nothing other than a cool shower and her comfy couch.

"How was your day, Finley?" his dad asked at the dinner table.

Finn slurped up a noodle covered in tomato sauce and Parmesan cheese. "It was good. We decided to round off the seat and backrest for the throne. That kept us busy today. Now all we need to do is assemble them together then attach the legs and armrests. Maybe we'll add some decor or something afterwards; but it should be easy going from now on."

"Glad to hear it." Mr. Davidson smiled at his son's excitement.

"What was the first thing you built by yourself, Dad?"

"Let's see…" He thought it over. "I think it was a birdhouse. No, it was a little shelf with a hook to hang your keys on."

Finley smirked to himself. *A throne is much harder to make than a shelf. Maybe I'm better at construction than Dad was at my age.* "Did you have any help?" he asked.

"Your grandmother helped me with the measurements and math," Mr. Davidson answered. "The rest I did myself. It wasn't the prettiest shelf but it was functional and I was proud of it."

His mom added, "It's the shelf that holds all of your grandparent's family albums, Finley."

"I made that shelf as a Father's Day present," Mr. Davidson specified. "I never expected him to keep it for this many years."

Finley frowned. "Wait, are you talking about the crooked shelf in their basement?"

His dad laughed. "It hangs crooked because I made the shelf crooked. If they'd hung it up straight, everything would slide off."

"It certainly has character." Finley's mom chuckled.

"I guess my throne will have some too," Finn admitted, "but it'll be functional."

She asked, "Are you and Leah going to work on it after supper?"

"No, we're both pretty tired from today's work."

Mr. Davidson rinsed off his plate at the sink and glanced out the window. "Finley, why did you leave everything out?"

He looked at his dad in confusion. "What?"

"You left all the tools out on the lawn. Even the handsaw isn't put away. Do you know how dangerous that is?"

Finley watched his father's face grow red and knew he was in big trouble.

"If anyone saw them out there—" He stopped himself before going on. "Call Leah. I need to speak with both of you about this."

Finley got up without a word. He could tell now wasn't the time to hesitate or ask questions.

"Leah," he spoke rapidly on the phone, "you need to come over, now."

"Finn, I'm exhausted. We agreed to keep working tomorrow."

"It's not that. We're in trouble and my dad wants you to come over."

"Really?"

"Dad is M-A-D."

"What did we do? I—"

He interrupted, "Just come. Now."

His dad was waiting for him at the back door. "Is she coming?"

"Yes."

"Good. We'll wait for her outside. Come on."

Finley followed his father to the backyard and stood among the scattered wood and tools on the ground. It hadn't looked messy until then. Even the seat and backrest looked a little trashy. Leah arrived quickly and fidgeted nervously beside him.

"Thank you for coming, Leah," Mr. Davidson said. "Do you know why I asked you over?"

She shook her head timidly.

He continued. "This yard is a mess and the worst part is you left all of my tools on the ground. I don't have a problem with you borrowing them but I do take issue with the condition they're in now."

Finley kept his eyes on the ground. He didn't dare look in his father's eyes.

"When you're on a worksite, you need to keep everything tidy," Mr. Davidson explained. "Partially because then you'll know where everything is and can quickly access it but it's also for your safety. Look at the handsaw," he said, directing their attention to where it lay on the ground. "What would happen if someone was walking and didn't see it? They could cut their shoe, or worse, their bare foot. There's a hammer here," he said, pointing, "and one over there. That's an easy way to trip or stub your toe. Medical bills are expensive and your health and safety are important. Do you understand?"

Finley and Leah nodded.

"After you've finished work, you always need to clean up, even if you're just taking a break. What if a stranger found all of these tools on the lawn, with no one around to claim them? It's not the same as leaving a beach ball lying around. These tools are expensive and someone could steal them. Don't get me wrong, we live in a safe neighborhood but anyone can make a mistake, especially if they think they can get away with it. If someone is struggling to do the right thing, I don't want to unintentionally tempt them to make the wrong decision. Do you understand?"

"Yes. Sorry, Dad."

Leah nodded. "Sorry, Mr. Davidson."

Finn added, "We won't do it again."

His dad crossed his arms. "OK. Thank you for the apology. Now, how are you going to fix the situation?"

Finn said, "We'll clean up everything."

His dad asked, "And tomorrow? What will you do?"

Leah answered, "We'll clean up everything when we're done or before we take a break."

Mr. Davidson nodded, approvingly. "And I don't want to see the handsaw on the ground again. If you're done using it, you can lay it on the sawhorse or put it back in the garage."

"Yes sir," Finn said.

"You're good kids," his father said, uncrossing his arms. "You're learning… Sometimes I forget what I haven't taught you yet. With that in mind, I'm sorry for not explaining this sooner."

The kids nodded together, accepting his apology.

"I'm just glad no one was hurt," he said, before walking back inside.

Finley and Leah looked at each other then silently got to work. They put all the tools in their correct places in the garage and piled the wood in the far corner.

"Sorry for dragging you into one of my dad's lectures," Finley apologized, after they finished.

"No, I deserved it," Leah said. "We both left the mess and we both needed the lesson. See you tomorrow."

"Ten again?"

"Yeah."

15

It was about ten-thirty by the time Leah made it to Finley's backyard.

"Hi," he greeted.

"Hey. Sorry I'm late. I must've forgotten to turn on my alarm last night."

Finley waved it off. "No problem."

"Whatcha doin'?"

"I've been looking through the rest of our scrap wood and separating the pieces we can use for the legs and armrests. They're already measured; we just have to cut them. How are your arms today?"

Leah rubbed them. "They're feeling better, a little sore but not too bad."

"Do you want to saw first today?"

"Sure."

She cut four planks for the legs then he cut the wood for the armrests.

"I've been thinking of a couple different ways to attach the seat to the backrest," he said as he slapped a mosquito on his arm. "I think the best way is this." He held the backrest against the edge of the seat at a ninety-degree angle. "We can nail through the backrest, into the seat." He pointed at the area. "We can also add extra support by attaching a small piece of wood along the bottom of the backrest and under the seat but we'll have to be careful nailing these particular pieces together." He smirked.

Leah frowned. "Huh? Why?"

He explained, "Because, if a nail goes through the seat, it'll stab our butts when we sit down on the chair."

She guffawed. "Ouch. Then I'll let you take on the responsibility of hammering while I hold the seat and backrest together. If we get stabbed in the butt, we can blame you later."

He rolled his eyes. "It'll be fine." He grabbed a hammer and the bucket of nails, as Leah positioned the pieces together. The nails went in crooked because of the angle he was hitting them and one poked out awkwardly.

"Wait, keep holding everything together," he instructed.

He hammered the pointy end of the nail downward, into the wood. It stuck out from the wood in an ugly manner but at least it wouldn't hurt them or rip their clothing. Then he nailed a board underneath, along the edge where the seat and backrest joined.

"Done," he said with satisfaction. "Let go."

Leah obeyed. "It's working. It's staying together."

"Let's do the legs next," Finley suggested. "That way we can sit in it sooner."

He laid the chair on its side then positioned a leg next to it.

"Move it to the left a little," Leah instructed. "Yeah, right there." She hammered a nail through the seat, into the leg. "I'm going to put two nails in. It'll be more secure."

She nailed in the bottom two legs then Finley flipped the chair and she did the other two.

"I hope this works," she said as she attached the last leg. "I don't think the legs match up with each other very well. It doesn't look square."

"As long as they're the same length and it doesn't wobble, it'll be fine."

They set the chair on its legs. The ground was uneven, making it hard to see if it was balanced.

"Let's move it to the driveway," Leah advised.

The seat of the chair was parallel to the driveway but it didn't seem to rest very well upon the legs. The chair shifted uneasily but the legs remained planted on the ground.

"It's a little wobbly." Leah grimaced. "Something about the way they were attached isn't right."

"But can it hold our weight?" Finley asked, as he prepared to sit on it.

"Wait. First, double check that no nails are poking out."

He scanned the seat at eye-level. "It's all good." Carefully, he slid into the chair.

"Well?" Leah asked.

He wiggled around a little and lifted his feet off the ground. "It's good," he declared. "It's holding my weight. We did it."

"My turn, my turn." Leah bounced up and down, as he got out. She carefully sat down and sighed when it didn't collapse beneath her.

"We made a chair, by ourselves." Finn laughed.

"Wow." Leah laughed along.

"Now we gotta turn it into a throne," he said, calming down. "Armrests will help but, maybe, it needs more?"

"It's a pretty big chair," Leah reminded. "That alone makes it resemble a throne. At least, it does to me."

They carried it back to the lawn so they could attach the remaining pieces of wood.

"Do you have any ideas about connecting the armrests?" she asked.

He picked up a small block of wood. "We'll nail one of these to the side of the seat, vertically. Then we'll place a larger board on top of it, horizontally. Bingo. An armrest. We can make one for both sides of the chair."

Leah hovered the boards above the chair, envisioning the finished product. "Are you sure it'll fit? This armrest takes up about a third of the seat space."

Finley shrugged. "Let's start with one side and see how it looks afterward."

They followed his plan and realized that Leah's worries were correct. If they attached an armrest on the other side, they wouldn't have enough room to sit in the chair.

"It's not too bad," he said. "We can just have one armrest."

"It looks weird, though." Leah winced. "It looks as if we made a mistake and couldn't fix it and now it's leaning to one side."

"No it isn't."

"Yes it is, look at it from this angle."

He stood by her side and squinted at the throne. "Maybe a little," he admitted.

"Well? Now what?"

"What do you mean?"

"You're the leader of this project. What do we do now?"

He thought about it while scrutinizing their creation. It didn't have the appearance of a throne as he'd envisioned.

"I'll sit and think about it," he said, as he took a seat in the chair.

This time, the wood creaked loudly beneath him. He adjusted his weight to the opposite side and it creaked again.

"Finley, the chair is totally crooked now," Leah warned. "Maybe you should get up."

He took her suggestion and resumed standing beside her. The throne remained leaning to one side. The more Finley looked, the more dissatisfied he became. He began to realize the whole time he'd been working on the throne, he'd seen everything through a filter of optimism; but now, he was looking at it with a critical eye and felt displeased with the result. A couple nails were poking out of the wood, some of the edges they'd sawed were rough and jagged; he could tell where his measurements had been incorrect and where things had been nailed in a crooked fashion.

This isn't how I imagined it at all. His shoulders drooped as he said, "It looks as though it could fall apart any minute."

"I'm sorry, Finn. I don't know what we can do to fix it." She slapped him on the back. "But look. We built a throne and did it by ourselves."

"Yeah." He sat down on the grass and stared at it.

"Maybe we can add some more nails to the legs and the seat?" she suggested.

He changed the subject, tired of looking at his messy construct. "I'm hungry. Let's have some lunch."

They cleaned up the tools and scraps of unused wood but left the throne where it was. They were scared it would break apart if they moved it again.

"We have leftover meatloaf in the fridge," Leah mentioned. "Wanna come over and have some?"

"Nah, I think I'll stay here and have a sandwich."

"OK. Should I come by afterward and we can work some more?"

"Uh…" He rubbed his head. "I have a little headache. Maybe I should stay inside for the rest of the day. I think we're done building anyway. We can check this item off our summer list."

Leah knew he was upset because their throne didn't look nicer and was barely functional. She could tell he needed to be alone with his thoughts so she waved goodbye and went home; but she couldn't erase the memory of Finn's disappointment. She picked at her food during dinner with her family and wished she knew how to help make the throne better or, at least, make Finley feel better.

Maybe I'll come up with an idea if I get a good look at what's wrong with the throne, she thought, as she helped Diane clear the dining room table.

She let her mom know she was going to Finley's house for a little while then dashed over. She found Mr. Davidson standing over their project with his hands in his pockets and a pencil behind his ear.

"Hi, Mr. Davidson," she said as she approached him.

He turned around; looking as though he'd been caught doing something he shouldn't. "Hello, Leah. You scared me, I didn't hear you approach."

She chuckled. "Sorry. What are you doing?"

He turned back to the chair. "I was examining your handiwork."

"Yeah, we know it's not very good. Finn's kinda upset about it actually."

"Oh? He didn't mention it to me."

"I came over to see if I could somehow fix it."

"Oops. Speaking of Finley..." Mr. Davidson motioned to the kitchen window.

Finley suddenly disappeared from the kitchen window and emerged from the backdoor.

"Hey, Leah," he said as he walked over.

"Hey. I was just telling your dad I wanted to look at our throne some more. Maybe we can figure out a way to fix it?"

Finley shrugged. "It was just for fun. I don't care if it's good or not."

Leah frowned. "Of course you do. We both want it to be functional and, right now, we can't risk sitting on it because it'll probably fall apart."

"I could suggest some improvements, if you're interested," Mr. Davidson said.

Finley was going to refuse but Leah unintentionally interrupted him. "Seriously? We'll take them."

"This is a nice feature," he complimented, pointing to the backrest. "But if we add some wood glue between these planks and use a woodworking vise to hold them together while it dries, everything will be less ridged and we can sand down the edges—"

"I'm still not feeling very good." Finley motioned to his head. "I'm gonna rest inside."

"Are you sure?" Leah asked.

"Yeah, but you guys can work on it, if you want." He shuffled his feet all the way to the house.

Leah looked at Mr. Davidson. "Maybe…we can surprise him with a really nice throne?"

He smiled sadly. "I wish he'd join us."

"Maybe tomorrow he'll feel better."

Together they dismantled the work Leah and Finley had done over the past couple of days. Mr.

Davidson wanted to keep some of it intact but, upon further inspection, decided it was better to start from scratch. He showed Leah how to measure the pieces and explained the reason why screws held better than nails. He also showed how to saw through the wood effectively and drew a quick sketch, with Leah's guidance, of Finley's ideas for the throne. He suggested making the base a hollow cube. That would ensure steadiness and make it appear grander; however, they'd have to scrap Finley's hope of having a hexagon seat. Leah agreed to this, on his behalf. In just two hours, they had blueprints with all the measurements they needed and an assembled backrest.

"The wood glue will need to dry," Mr. Davidson explained. "For tonight, we can set the backrest on the garage floor and I'll leave my car parked on the street."

"It's getting late." Leah regarded the streetlights, which had just come on. "I should go home anyway. Thanks for all your help."

"You're welcome."

"Can you help tomorrow, too? I think Finn will like our plans."

"You have the blueprints and measurements. You're welcome to use any tool, as needed, and I'll help however I can, after work."

"Great. Thanks again." Leah waved as she walked home.

Mr. Davidson muttered, as he closed the garage door, "Hopefully my son will join us."

16

Leah stopped by Finley's house around 10 o'clock the next day and tried to recruit his help.

"Finn, come on. It was your idea in the first place. Why don't you want to work on the throne anymore?"

"We already did it," he explained, frowning. "We can scratch it off our list and move onto the next one." He showed her the Friday newspaper. "Look, next Wednesday the theater in the mall has an R-rated movie. We can go see it."

"But our throne wasn't good and you know that."

"The point was to make one by ourselves and have fun. It doesn't matter if it was good or bad."

"Is that why you went inside yesterday? 'Cause your dad was working on it with me?"

He hesitated. "Maybe."

"Finley, that's not fair. You said if we couldn't sit on it, we'd ask for help. That's what I did. Otherwise, I wouldn't have talked about it with your dad."

"But I did sit on it. We both did."

"It wasn't safe, though. We're lucky it didn't crash beneath us. Why is this such a big deal?"

He raised his voice in frustration. "It isn't. It isn't a big deal. We finished our goal and now we can move on."

Leah stared at him angrily. They rarely fought but when they did, it was ugly.

Finally, she burst out, "Whatever. You finished your job for the summer list but I didn't. I want to make something good, something we can use more than once before breaking apart. You can stay inside all day and I'll work on it by myself."

"Fine." He slammed the door in her face.

"Do I have your permission to go through your garage and use your dad's stuff?" she yelled through the door.

"I. Don't. Care." He stomped off.

He was furious with Leah. *How could she give up on our project? She and Dad destroyed it. They undid all of my hard work in less than an hour. She doesn't even have to say it; I know she likes Dad's work over mine. She proved it when she decided to work with him rather than me.* He walked aimlessly around the house. Every once in a while, he peeked out the window to see what Leah was doing but he couldn't find her. *She's probably working in the garage, making a mess and wrecking more of our stuff. I wish we hadn't made a throne in the first place. It started out fun but now it isn't worth it. First, Dad got mad at us, now Leah and I are in a fight. Plus, the new throne she and Dad are making will sit in the backyard, forever taunting me. I wasn't good enough. I couldn't do it without the help of 'daddy'. And Leah couldn't just have fun. She always wants everything to be perfect. Perfect edges, perfect nails in the perfectly cut wood. Whatever. Life isn't perfect. She better start getting used to it.*

Someone knocked on the door and he hurried out of eyesight from the kitchen window.

"Finn?" Leah shouted from the other side of the door, "Can you open the door? Please?"

He ignored her, grabbed a box of granola bars and scurried downstairs. Then he turned up the volume on the TV so he wouldn't be able to hear if she knocked again.

He filled the day by lounging on the couch and playing video games. It felt good to defeat something and be crowned a winner.

See? he thought, *I'm good at something.*

Around 5 o'clock, he heard his mother calling his name.

"What are you doing down here?" she asked, as she descended the stairs.

"I have a headache."

"Do you know Leah's outside, working?"

"Yeah, I told her she could work without me. I don't feel good enough to do anything today."

"I see." His mom paused, "Do you want some medication for it? Maybe if you feel better, you can join her."

He dismissed her advice. "Uh, maybe later. Thanks, Mom."

"He's not coming up, Peter," Mrs. Davidson told her husband when he got home from work. "He says he has a headache but I know something else is going on. I think he and Leah had a fight."

"It's a shame he's missing out," Mr. Davidson replied. "Leah's been working hard all day. She cut all the wood and seems to be enjoying the work."

"Well, we can't fix every problem our son has," she reasoned. "Sometimes Finley needs to learn things on his own."

"I agree, Jan. In the meantime, I told Leah I'd help finish the project. It would be a shame if I let her down, too."

Mrs. Davidson squeezed her husband's hand. "I'll call you when dinner's ready."

He strolled to the garage and looked at his blueprints. "I think we can finish today, if we put our minds to it. What do you say?"

Leah grinned. "Everything's cut and ready to assemble. Your instructions on using the sawhorse were extremely helpful. I had no problem cutting by myself."

"I'm very impressed by your work ethic. I can see you excelling in any career you choose. Perhaps carpentry?"

She laughed. "Maybe as a hobby."

He noticed a bandage on her hand. "What happened here?"

A flash of guilt crossed her face. "Oh, it's nothing. I got a splinter earlier and it started to bleed when I took it out. It's fine now."

Leah left out the part where she'd tried asking Finn for help but he didn't open the door for her. She had to go home to get a bandage. He'd hurt her more than the splinter.

"Did you clean it before putting on the bandage?"

"Yes."

"Good. We don't want it to become infected."

She pointed to the blueprints. "Where should we begin?"

"We can assemble the base together," he said.

"Great."

By the time Mrs. Davidson announced dinner was ready, they'd finished putting together the throne's base and backrest.

"Would you care to join us for dinner?" Mr. Davidson asked.

"No, thanks. My family's been trying to eat together more often so I should get going anyway. Can I come back after we finish?"

He nodded. "All that's left is assembling the armrests, which will take us a while. Now is a good time to take a break."

They resumed work around seven-thirty and finished the whole project by 9 o'clock.

"As I said yesterday," Mr. Davidson explained, "we'll need to let all the glue dry overnight so it stays together properly. Because the throne will stay outdoors, we'll need to waterproof the wood sometime soon but tomorrow you'll have the honor of sitting on it for the first time."

"I've learned a lot from you, Mr. Davidson. Thanks for all your help; I can't wait to try this out."

"I'm glad we had enough supplies to make it." He motioned to the few remaining scraps of wood. "We could add these as a few decorative pieces, if you like."

Leah shook her head. "I like it just the way it is."

The bottom of the chair was squared off but they'd rounded off the corners of the armrests and created a regal arch at the top of the backrest. Its simplistic design showed the natural beauty of the wood grain.

"Well, I suppose that concludes our work together. It's been a pleasure." He held out his hand and Leah shook it.

They left the throne to dry underneath the tree house. Before the sun rose the next morning, Leah scurried to the Davidson's backyard. Wrapped in a blanket and seated upon the throne, she watched the sunrise. The stars slowly disappeared and the clouds turned from red to yellow to white.

"God, you paint the best skies," she whispered.

As she continued watching, she thought about the past week. She'd learned so much during that time. Not just about how to make something new from a pile of wood but about herself too. *I never thought I could make something this cool or enjoy building it as much as I did. Now I feel ready for the next, new, big thing in my life. High school. I'm tougher and stronger than I was last week; I can handle anything.*

Her conversation with Diane had made her a little nervous about the kids there but now she felt prepared for it. In the same way she had worked on the throne, she'd tackle one challenge at a time. *And if I need help, I'll take it.*

Leah and Finn's List for an Awesome Summer

1. ~~Eat a whole gallon of ice cream (each)~~

2. ~~Build a throne~~

3. Take a dance class

4. ~~Hunt crabs at night, at the beach~~

5. Sneak into an R rated movie at the theater

6. Drive a car

7. Discover a new world

8. ~~Stay awake for 24 hours straight~~

9. ~~Find buried treasure~~

10. ~~Attempt a world record~~

17

"I don't know if you're still mad at me but this may be our only chance to do it," Leah said to Finley on the phone.

Five days had passed since they last spoke to one another and they were running out of time.

"You said it yourself, it's time to complete the next item on our summer list," she continued, "and there's an R-rated movie playing tomorrow. Are you in?"

Finley silently contemplated the situation. Leah was right. Tomorrow was probably the only opportunity they had. Besides, he was tired of fighting. He wanted things to go back to normal. The past few days had been miserable. Every time he looked out the back window, he saw the throne she'd made with his dad. It looked pretty good but it was also a reminder of his failure and Leah had chosen his dad over him. The memory still stung.

"Finn?"

He relented. "Yeah, OK. Let's do it. What's the movie called, again?"

"I don't remember but there's a kid's movie playing at the same time. I heard Diane ask Mom if she can use the car tomorrow, which is perfect. She'll hang out with her friends at the mall and we'll go to the theater."

"But we can't get into an R-rated movie without a grownup."

"We'll get tickets to the kid's movie then after it, starts we'll sneak into the other one."

"Huh…" He pondered the idea. "That could actually work but you're terrible at lying. Can we get away with this?"

"Because we'll see the kid's movie first…technically, I didn't lie when I asked Mom if I could go."

"I guess that makes sense."

"Come over around six-thirty. The movie starts at seven."

"All right."

Finley followed the plan the next day. He wasn't ready to completely forgive Leah but he was willing to put it aside so they could enjoy the night. Her family was going to the cabin next week and he didn't want an argument hanging over their heads the whole time she was gone. Meanwhile, Leah felt the same way. *I still don't understand why he's been so angry about the throne. I refuse to accept I did anything wrong but I'm willing to put the argument behind me. I want my friend back and that's more important to me than an argument.*

She greeted him at the door. "Great, you're on time. Diane, Finn's here. We're ready to go."

"Just a sec," Diane called from the bathroom. She'd spent the last half hour carefully spraying her hair and layering on mascara.

"Does she know our plan?" Finley whispered to Leah.

She bit her lip. "No way. She'd bust us for sure."

"Hello, Finley." Mrs. Harris entered the room. "I haven't seen you much this summer. What's been keeping you busy?"

"Hi, Mrs. Harris. I've, uh, been busy with a couple projects. Nothing too interesting, though."

"Diane," Leah called again. "We're gonna be late."

Diane tossed a purse over her shoulder, as she walked out the front door. "I'm ready, Leah. Sheesh, don't have a tantrum. Bye, Mom."

"Have fun." Mrs. Harris waved goodbye as they drove off.

"You guys know the rules by now," Diane said, as she turned on her right signal light. "I drop you off at the theater and pick you up five minutes after it ends. What time does it finish?"

Leah hadn't thought to check when the children's movie would be over. Before she could answer, Finley spoke up.

"About nine-thirty."

"Fine. We'll meet at the theater entrance. Got it?"

Leah nodded. "Yep, and thanks for driving us, Diane."

"It worked out perfectly." Finley smiled, secretively.

"Yeah, whatever," Diane replied. "If I'm late meeting you guys there, just stay at the entrance. OK?"

"We'll be fine, Diane," Leah insisted.

"You have the money for the tickets, right?" Finley whispered to Leah.

"Uh-huh," she replied, "I already gave it to Diane."

"Because she's our backup alibi. If my parents ask about tonight, I'll say we went to a kids' movie and she'll explain she got our tickets. There's no reason for anyone to suspect what we're up to."

You're maniacally brilliant when you want to be."

After finding a parking spot, the three of them walked to the ticket counter.

Diane spoke to the ticket salesman. "Two tickets for…" She paused and asked Leah, "What movie are you guys watching?"

Leah quickly scanned the movie posters. "*The Land Before Time*."

"*The Land Before*—that's what you want to watch?"

"Yes," Finley lied. "It's a good movie. It's…sentimental."

Leah averted her eyes and nodded in agreement.

Diane frowned in confusion and looked at the movie posters. *Something weird is going on but I can't tell what it is. The only other movie listed is way too violent and it's rated R; Leah would never watch it.* She shrugged. "Two tickets for *The Land Before Time*, please."

Leah and Finley took their tickets, said goodbye to Diane and walked in.

"Do you want popcorn or a soda?" Finley asked as they passed the concession stand.

"I'm too nervous to eat anything." Leah gulped.

"Tickets, please." A worker in black pants and a red vest held out his hand.

"Huh? Oh, here." Leah handed hers over to him. She was sweating. *Everyone will see through our act. They'll totally suspect a couple of teens going to see a children's movie.*

"Here you are." He handed the ticket back after punching a hole through it. "And you?"

Finley handed his over, trying to act casual. *Does anyone know our plan? How often do teens try to sneak into an R-rated movie anyway?*

"Here you go," the worker said, handing the punched ticket back. "Please make your way to theater room one and enjoy the movie."

Leah and Finley felt as though they were floating as they took their seats at the back of the theater.

"I think we can do it," Leah whispered.

"We've made it this far," Finley agreed. "There's no turning back now."

"I wonder why movies are rated R anyway," she mentioned carelessly. "I've never thought about it before."

The lights suddenly dimmed and a movie preview started playing, advertising another children's movie.

"I'll stay here for ten minutes then sneak out," Leah said. "Wait here for a bit then follow me. I'll meet you in the hallway, by the bathrooms."

"If we get caught, will we be kicked out?" Finley asked.

Leah shrugged. "Maybe; or they'll check our tickets and make us come back here. I don't know."

They sat still, silently counting down the minutes until time was up. Leah nodded to Finn then snuck out, undetected. He counted to one hundred then followed. When he looked down the hall, however, he couldn't see Leah. A theater attendant passed by and Finley tried to act casual by meandering to the men's room. Just before he reached it, Leah emerged from the women's room.

She sighed in relief when she saw him. "Sorry. I was afraid someone would see me waiting in the hall and get suspicious. The only place I knew I could hide was the bathroom."

He covered his mouth to keep from laughing.

She raised an eyebrow. "It's not that funny. Come on, let's go."

They tiptoed to the other theater room and found two seats in the back. Everyone was too engrossed in the movie to notice.

"I can't believe we did it," Finley whispered. "We snuck into an R-rated movie."

Leah's excitement shone in her eyes, although it was too dark for Finley to notice. "I hope it's a good one."

Unfortunately, after watching the film for about twenty minutes, neither of them was enjoying themselves. The scenes were riddled with violence and gore. Several times Finn wanted to cover his eyes but was too embarrassed to do so in front of Leah. He didn't realize she felt the same way about the situation. The characters swore a lot and each time one was uttered the kids were stunned. Of course, they'd heard that type of language at school but never to that amount or spoken so angrily. Unknowingly to each of them, the worst was yet to come. In the next scene, the main character was kissing his girlfriend…and then it got worse. The 'adult content' portion of the movie made their cheeks burn and sitting side by side, a boy and a girl, was much too embarrassing for either of them to endure. They realized together they uncomfortable watching such mature content and Leah's spirit of adventure was the first to break.

"I have to pee," she said to Finn.

He jumped at the opportunity to leave. "Me too."

They quickly left the room and hid in the adjacent bathrooms. Finley splashed cold water on his face and stared at himself in the mirror. He wasn't sure he could even look at Leah without his cheeks turning red. *Taking health class in school was bad enough but this is way worse. Leah's my best friend and she's a girl. I mean…I don't want to kiss her or anything but now, I'll never be able to look at her the same way again.* He felt as if the movie had ruined a piece of their friendship; the innocence they used to have was gone. They used to just overlook their differences, pretend they didn't exist but now it would be impossible. *I'm glad she's going to the cabin in a few days. I need a break from her. It'll help me forget what just happened.*

Meanwhile, Leah had locked herself in a stall and was calming herself down by breathing slowly. She couldn't erase certain images from her mind and was trying to focus on something else, anything else. *My hands are clammy. The stall door is cold. I have popcorn stuck to the bottom of my shoe. I wish I'd just stayed home. How am I going to get out of this mess? I can't admit to Finley how uncomfortable I am. He'll think I'm five years old but I also can't go through with watching the rest of the movie.* She exhaled slowly. *OK, I'll at least admit I hated the gore…but I won't mention the other parts. It's way too awkward to talk about.* She soaked a square of paper towel in cold water and brought it to her face, to cool off. When she exited the room, Finley was waiting for her in the hall.

"Hey," he said.

"Hey…" Her voice wavered slightly. "I was thinking…I don't really want to watch the rest of the movie. It has way too much blood and grossness for my taste."

"Oh, uh, yeah," he stuttered. "It's not even an interesting movie. People dying and blood flying everywhere isn't much of a plot. You want to get some ice cream at the food court instead?"

"Diane might see us if we leave the theater early."

He awkwardly shoved his hands in his pockets. "Oh, right. I guess…we could go back to the kid's movie?"

"OK."

They took their original seats in theater room one and watched the rest of the children's movie in silence. Half the time their minds drifted back to the R-rated movie but the lightheartedness of the kid's movie reminded them of the simpler, happier times of childhood and they were unexpectedly comforted by it. They exited the room after the credits ended. Neither one knew what to say to the other so they awkwardly looked around, silently wishing Diane would hurry and pick them up. In twenty-five minutes, she was there. It was the longest twenty-five minutes of their lives.

"Ready to go?" Diane asked as she approached with two of her friends.

"Yep," Leah said.

"Cool. Joelle and Gabriela need a ride home so they're coming with us. Finley, that means you'll be dropped off last because you live so close to us."

He gulped. "Sure."

Gabriela sat in the front with Diane while the rest crammed into the back. Leah and Finley sat as narrowly as they could, not even letting their feet touch. Normally they wouldn't notice but that night they noticed everything. As soon as Joelle left, Leah moved to the empty seat and they both breathed easier.

"Thanks for the ride," Finley said, as they stopped in front of his house. He avoided eye contact with Leah. "I guess I'll see you…after you get back from the cabin?"

She nodded. "Yeah, I still have to pack and help get everything ready before we go so I probably won't have time to see you before we leave."

"Right. Well, see you around. I mean, you know, bye."

She waved half-heartedly. "Bye."

After he left, Diane glanced back at her sister. "Um…OK. Is it just me or was that awkward?"

Leah answered quickly, "No."

"All right."

"We're just tired. It's been a long day."

Diane pulled into their driveway. "How was the movie?"

"Fine."

"Nothing interesting happened?"

Leah's mind raced, trying to come up with an answer to stop Diane from asking any more questions. Finally, she said, "You're right. We were too old for that movie."

Leah and Finn's List for an Awesome Summer

1. ~~Eat a whole gallon of ice cream (each)~~
2. ~~Build a throne~~
3. Take a dance class
4. ~~Hunt crabs at night, at the beach~~
5. ~~Sneak into an R rated movie at the theater~~
6. Drive a car
7. Discover a new world
8. ~~Stay awake for 24 hours straight~~
9. ~~Find buried treasure~~
10. ~~Attempt a world record~~

18

Leah was groggy when she woke up on Monday. Even though she'd gone to bed early the night before, it had taken her a while to fall asleep because of her excitement to go to the cabin. She'd spent the whole weekend prepping. On Friday she'd gone back to the town library and checked out a couple books. On Saturday she got some of her art stuff together in a box, including the shells and beach glass she collected with Finn and, after church on Sunday, she packed all her clothes and essentials for the two-week trip.

The glowing, red numbers on her alarm clock read six-thirty.

"Good morning," Mrs. Harris said, as Leah shuffled to the bathroom.

"G'morn," she mumbled back.

"Dear, you didn't sleep well last night, did you?"

Leah shook her head and closed the door. The warm shower helped wake her up but her eyelids were still droopy, when she entered the kitchen.

"Your father is out getting us some breakfast," her mom explained.

Memories of cleaning out the fridge and eating leftovers the night before sprang to Leah's mind. "Oh, right," she said and grabbed a seat at the table.

"No, I'm back," Mr. Harris said, as he entered the kitchen with a bag of bagels and a container of fruit salad.

Leah bit into a bagel without cutting it or spreading anything on it. "Yum," she said between bites.

"They're still warm." Mrs. Harris chewed.

"That's what happens when you're up this early." Mr. Harris smiled. "Where's Diane?"

A groan sounded from the hallway.

"She's having a hard time waking up this early," Mrs. Harris said, as she eyed Leah. "They both are."

Leah grumbled, "We're teenagers. Of course it's hard."

"I'll start loading the car while you finish eating," Mr. Harris said.

"Aren't you hungry, Steven?" Mrs. Harris asked.

"I'll eat on the way there," he replied.

Half an hour later, they began their three-hour drive to the cabin. Leah and Diane fell asleep soon after they got onto the freeway. They'd been lulled by the soft jazz music on the radio and white noise of tires on pavement. By the time Leah awoke, the gray industrial landscape was replaced by lush, green foliage and fields.

She blinked sleepily and asked, "How much farther?"

Her mother glanced back. "A little under an hour."

"If I remember correctly," her father added, "there's a gas station about thirty miles ahead. We'll stop there for gasoline and a bathroom break."

"OK." She rested her head back and watched the landscape float by.

They were on the outskirts of a series of rolling hills when they found the station.

"Hi, folks," the clerk greeted them through the car window.

"Hi." Leah's dad smiled politely. "Fill it up, please."

"Sure thing. Do you want your windows washed and motor oil checked, while I'm at it?"

Mr. Harris nodded. "Thanks."

Mrs. Harris asked, "Is there a bathroom we can use?"

The clerk pointed. "Yep, that door over there."

She thanked the clerk and left the vehicle. Leah followed but Diane stayed behind, still asleep.

After stopping by the bathroom, they roamed around the store as the clerk finished washing the windows.

"Mom, can I have something to drink?" Leah asked.

"Yes. I'm thirsty too. What looks good?"

"There's juice here," Leah mentioned, "and a coffee pot over there."

Mr. Harris and the clerk entered the store and wandered over to the counter.

"So, where are you folks headed?" the clerk asked.

"We're staying at a cabin not too far from here," Mrs. Harris explained, as she set two cups of coffee and two bottles of apple juice on the counter.

The clerk punched in a couple numbers on the till. "Oh, you're on vacation?"

Mr. Harris paid him. "Yes, sir."

"Well, that's fantastic." The clerk smiled. "We definitely see lots of new faces around at this time of year; most are doing the same thing as you folks. Sometimes, in autumn, people drive around here to enjoy the colorful leaves as well."

"That's a lovely idea. Perhaps we should do it, Steven," Mrs. Harris said.

He smiled at his wife. "We could have a little weekend road trip for our wedding anniversary."

"Are you familiar with the roads and trails around here?" the clerk asked.

"No, it's been several years since we last visited," Mr. Harris explained.

"Take this." The clerk handed him a large pamphlet. "It's got several maps in it. It shows the little dirt roads that lead to the cabins close by, the walking trials available and a few sightseeing areas."

Mr. Harris held out a ten-dollar bill. "That'll be very helpful, thank you."

The clerk waved his hand. "No need to pay. It's all a part of the service."

"Thank you very much." Mrs. Harris smiled.

"If you need anything else, be sure to give us a call." The clerk gave her the station's business card.

She tucked it in her bag. "We will. Have a nice day."

"You, too," the clerk called out, as they left.

Diane was awake when they returned to the car. She asked, "Are we almost there?"

"Yes," her dad replied.

Mrs. Harris navigated from the map, as Mr. Harris drove. They wound along the paved highway until they saw a little green sign with an arrow on it.

"Turn here," she instructed and they drove onto a gravel road.

It was surrounded by thick, tall trees. At every quarter mile, a little turnoff road emerged and seemed to lead to nowhere.

"Why are there so many little roads here?" Leah asked.

Her father explained, "They're driveways, leading to other cabin sites. They're long so you can't hear any traffic noise at the cabins."

They followed the snake-like road for several miles until Mrs. Harris pointed right. "This is the driveway. Number seven-one-seven."

"Good thing we had the map," Mr. Harris said as he turned the steering wheel. "I forgot how deep into the woods the cabin is and the trees look so much taller since the last time we were here; I don't know if we could have found it otherwise."

"Yes," Mrs. Harris agreed. "It certainly looks different."

"I'm hungry," Diane mumbled. "What time is it?"

"Ten-thirty," Leah said, only half paying attention to her sister.

They entered a small clearing with a cabin resting in the center. It had a porch with a large swing attached and a bird feeder hanging in front of a window. On the yard lay a small flower garden and a lawn table with four matching chairs. The chestnut brown logs of the cabin matched the surrounding trees and Leah imagined, on cloudy days, the roof camouflaged itself into the sky.

"I forgot it has so many windows," Diane commented.

Leah secretly thought, *The throne at Finn's place would fit perfectly here.*

"Let's get unpacked," Mr. Harris said, as he parked. "We can eat after we get settled in."

"Perhaps we should roast hot dogs and marshmallows tonight." Mrs. Harris smiled. "We haven't done that in ages."

"Leah did at Joy's party," Diane reminded.

"It's not the same," Leah argued. "That was a bonfire and most of our stuff burned anyway."

Diane dismissed her sister. "Whatever, a fire's a fire."

Leah grabbed her bag and changed the subject. "Ah, this is how fabric softener is supposed to smell."

"Pine and fresh leaves," her dad said, with a smile.

"Wait until it rains." Her mom's eyes sparkled. "There's nothing that compares to it."

Leah followed her into the cabin and two things caught her attention immediately; everything looked and smelled of wood.

She thought *I feel like I'm in a pioneer home, at a museum.*

"There are three bedrooms upstairs," her dad explained. "You can choose which one you want but leave the master bedroom for us."

"OK." Leah scampered upstairs before her sister had a chance to pick first. After peering into each room, she chose the one with a window facing the backyard. She could see four more lawn chairs surrounding a fire pit but what she found most intriguing were the trees. As she stared at them, they took on a mystical quality. Their leaves glowed in the sunlight and near the ground their shaded trunks appeared to be holding secrets. She tried counting all the trees but it seemed as though new ones kept popping up from the ground, making her lose count. She knew she was going to like it here.

"Ha, ha." Diane poked her head in the doorway. "I got the biggest room."

"Mom and Dad got the master bedroom so they got the biggest," Leah corrected, annoyed at her sister for disrupting her daydream.

Diane ignored her comment. "Your room is tiny compared to mine and I have a bigger closet."

"Congratulations," Leah mumbled.

"Mom and Dad are making sandwiches for lunch," Diane called, as she walked away.

You got the bigger room but I got the better one. Leah smiled at the trees.

She bounded down the stairs and found everyone else standing in the kitchen, preparing their meal.

Her mother sliced an orange and asked, "Leah, would you care to go on a short hike after lunch?"

"Cool," she said, as she grabbed the sliced ham and bread. "Where are we going?"

"The map shows a path leading to an old well," her father explained. "It's the closest sightseeing destination."

"Are you coming, Diane?" Mrs. Harris asked.

She grimaced. "Do I have to?"

"No."

"Then maybe I'll go another day," Diane answered.

Mr. Harris cautioned, "There isn't much to do around here alone. You might get bored."

Diane replied, "I'm still tired from getting up so early; besides, I want to explore the place some more."

Her parents looked at each other and shrugged.

Her mom said, "All right. Enjoy."

Before they left, Leah put on her favorite baseball cap then grabbed a water bottle and apple. Outside, she found her dad with the pamphlet.

"Where does the trail start?" she asked.

He pointed to the map. "If we cross the dirt road here, we should be able to find the trail about here."

Sure enough, they found the path tucked away among the trees, right where the map said.

"I expected more sunlight but the trees cover so much," her mom said, as she looked up at the arching branches above. "It doesn't even feel hot."

Leah tripped over a hidden root among the dirt and fallen leaves.

"Watch your step," her father reminded.

Other than an occasional root, the terrain was fairly level. Leah was used to the hard, hot sidewalks back home but this path was spongy and cool.

"What kind of tree is that?" she asked.

"I think it's a juniper," her mom answered.

"This one's a chokecherry," her dad said as he approached it and plucked a small group of cherries. He popped one into his mouth and offered them to Leah. "Want one?"

She took one.

"Careful you don't bite into the seed," he said as he spat his out.

She bit into it and winced. It was sour.

Her dad chuckled. "I guess they're not quite ripe yet. Still a little sour?"

She nodded and spat the rest out. Her tongue felt oddly dry afterward so she sipped her water.

"Strange sensation, isn't it?" her mother asked, eating her own handful of cherries.

"Yeah. I guess that's why they're called choke cherries."

Mrs. Harris chuckled. "If you cook them into a pie or jam, they don't leave that dry feeling on your tongue."

Leah refused her father's proffered hand with more cherries.

"I think I'll stick with blueberries," she said.

It took about an hour to get to their destination. The stone well had a little plaque in front, which read:

This well was once the property of Rimmington School. Documentation estimates the school was constructed in the early 1900s; however, in 1942, a malfunction in the school's heating system led to a fire, which destroyed the entire building. Funds were insufficient to rebuild, leading to a union with their neighbouring town. Bigweld School was in operation in 1943. Folklore depicts the well as a wishing well, referring to an earlier time when a student dropped a coin in the well for good luck. Lore states this action saved the lives of the staff and students from the fire. The well remains as a historical monument.

"I didn't know a school used to be here." Mr. Harris looked around.

"That would explain the small clearing over there." Mrs. Harris motioned to the area.

Leah rested her hands on the edge of the well and peered down. "I wonder how deep this goes." She reached down and touched the cool stones with her hand.

"Deep enough that if you fell, you'd be seriously hurt," her father cautioned.

Leah backed away from the edge but continued to look down. "Hello." Her voice echoed as it sank deeper than she could ever reach.

"Oh, look over here," her mom said, bending over a nearby patch of dirt.

"What is it?" Leah asked as she joined her mother's side.

"Deer tracks," Mrs. Harris answered.

Leah glanced at her then back at the tracks. "Deer live in these woods?"

"The woods provide shelter from the weather as well as camouflage," her mom explained.

"Have you ever seen one?" Leah asked.

"No," she admitted.

Her dad nodded. "One time, I saw one when I was camping with your grandfather."

"Do you think we'll get to see one?" she asked, in an excited voice.

"I don't know," her dad replied. "They're pretty good at hiding and they're easier to see after it's snowed."

"There must be other animals around," her mom continued. "Maybe coyotes or foxes, owls or hawks. Definitely mice."

Leah's smile grew bigger. "We never see any of those back home."

"But," her father interrupted, "it's also a good reminder to be careful. I don't think any of us should go hiking alone in case we encounter a dangerous animal."

Leah shrugged. "I hadn't planned on it anyway. No way am I getting lost by myself."

They made their way back with plenty of time before nightfall and found Diane reclining on the porch swing, reading a magazine.

"Did you have a good time?" her mom asked as they approached.

"Yeah." Diane closed her magazine. "A couple things brought back memories. Playing tag among the trees and Uncle Marv sweeping in the kitchen—but I don't know why I'd remember that."

Mrs. Harris laughed. "Oh, that's right. Do you remember, Steven?"

He looked confused.

She elaborated, "He was trying to make pancakes one morning but the bag of flour slipped from the counter and exploded everywhere. I think he still has flour in his hair."

"Wait…" Diane paused. "Is that why I remember the floor being slippery?"

Her mother's good nature abruptly ended. "Yes. We weren't impressed with you, young lady. You were sliding all over the floor. We had to toss away your socks because they were caked in flour."

"Oh, I remember those socks." Mr. Harris crossed his arms. "What a mess."

Leah wished she could join in but she didn't remember any of it. It was a downside of being the youngest child. Still, she enjoyed listening to them laugh and reminisce.

"I'm gonna grab a sweater," she announced once everyone had settled down.

"Yes, it's getting a little chilly," Mrs. Harris agreed.

"And dark," Mr. Harris added. "We should get the fire pit set up while there's still enough sunlight."

"I'll help, Dad," Diane offered, "but first, I'll get a sweater too."

Up in her bedroom, Leah gazed out the window again. The enchantment of the trees had turned dark and mysterious. *They're dancing, with their branches waving in the wind...and at the stroke of midnight, they'll pick up their roots from the ground and have a masquerade ball.*

As Leah was pulling on her sweater, she heard a little clatter from inside her closet. She looked over. *What was that? Did something fall off a hanger? Or was it a mouse?*

She tiptoed to the closet and reached out a hand to open the door. Suddenly, the door flung wide open and her sister jumped out.

"Boo," Diane yelled.

Leah screamed in her face and almost fell backward.

Diane laughed. "Got you."

"Wha—how did you—" Leah stammered.

"This is one of the things I found this afternoon." She motioned for Leah to take a better look at the back panel of her closet. "It slides open, see? It joins our closets together. Probably so there's extra storage space if there's only one guest staying here."

Leah frowned. "New rule. No more entering the other person's room through the closet."

Diane rolled her eyes. "Duh. This gag was good for one jump scare. Now that it's done, there's no need to ever use it again."

"Shake on it." Leah held her hand out.

Diane scoffed but shook it.

Back outside, their dad had already stacked wood into the fire pit and was just starting to light it. It took a few tries but once the larger pieces started to burn, he knew the fire would last a while.

"Your mother's collecting the food," he said as his daughters approached.

"We could move the table from the front yard, to back here," Diane suggested. "Then we can prepare our food on it."

Her father nodded. "Leah, why don't you help your sister?"

"Sure, Dad."

The two of them returned just in time for their mother to place the food on it. The tabletop was covered with an assortment of condiments, hot dog buns, sausages, a bag of marshmallows, cans of soda, bottles of water, a bowl of coleslaw and a bag of cheese puffs.

"A feast for a king," Mr. Harris said, grandly. "Thank you, my dear. Where are the roasting sticks?"

"I couldn't find them," she answered.

Diane remarked, "I saw them in the kitchen pantry. I'll get them."

"Thank you, Diane," he said.

A few moments later, everyone was huddled together. The fire crackled, sausage sizzled and birds tweeted.

"I can't hear any vehicles," Leah said quietly. "It's weird."

"No one's around for at least a quarter of a mile," her mom reminded.

"Sometimes I wish we lived in the country," her dad said, "away from everyone and the busy atmosphere."

"We're not moving, are we Dad?" Diane asked.

"No," he said reassuringly. "It would be very inconvenient for us to move to the countryside and it would require some extra work to maintain."

Mrs. Harris grimaced. "Such as sewage control and yard work."

"And we'd have to drive farther to work and school." Mr. Harris added.

"That's what makes this place so great," Mrs. Harris said. "It's a taste of that kind of life, without the work."

"Remind me to thank my brother again when we're home," he said, winking.

"How much does it cost to have a cabin?" Diane asked.

"A lot more than you think," her mom replied.

"Why don't we come here more often?" Leah asked.

Her parents looked at each other. Finally, her father said, "I don't know. We're usually busy or I take my vacation days throughout the year so we don't have time to stay for too long."

"It's a bit of a drive," their mother added. "And it involves a lot of planning and preparation."

"We could help," Diane offered.

"Yeah," Leah agreed.

"Maybe we should make this an annual trip," their dad suggested.

"Or, at the very least, every couple years," their mom said. "We could try different things other years. Perhaps we'll go on a road trip and visit your grandparents."

"We can't afford expensive trips," Mr. Harris reminded his daughters.

"We know," Leah shrugged, "but we don't need it to be expensive. It's nice just getting out of the house together."

"Yes, it is," said her parents, in unison.

They happily chatted the night away, sharing their hopes and plans for the rest of their two-week stay. That night became one of the sweetest memories Leah would have for years to come. It wasn't particularly special but it was meaningful because they were all happy and appreciative of one another in the peaceful atmosphere.

19

It hadn't even been a week since Leah and her family went to the cabin and Finley was home alone, bored out of his mind. He'd been thinking about calling his buddy Bryce for the past couple days but kept putting it off because it was hot outside and took so long to bike to his house. Today, however, Finn's reluctance was overpowered by his desire to hang out with a friend. He called him mid-morning. After it rang for the third time, he started to worry Bryce was still asleep.

"Hello?"

"Hey…Bryce?"

"Hey, Finn. How's it going?"

"It's good, dude. I didn't recognize your voice at first. Guess it's been a while since we talked on the phone."

Bryce chuckled. "Yeah, we usually meet up at school."

"Are you busy today?"

"Nah. Wanna come over?"

Finn smirked. Bryce was always inviting people over. He argued there was more to do near his house because he lived in the middle of the city. Finn suspected the true reason was because he didn't want to walk or bike all the way to someone else's place.

"Sure. I'll come right over. Be there in about forty-five minutes."

"Sweet. See you soon."

As estimated, Finley arrived almost exactly forty-five minutes later. He was tired, hot and sweaty but excited to see his friend.

"Whoa, it's a bajillion degrees outside," Bryce said as he opened the door and was greeted with a wave of heat.

"Hello to you, too." Finn breathed heavily.

"Come in, I'll get you some water."

"Thanks." He entered the house and looked around. "Hey, your cousin is coming over soon, isn't he?"

Bryce handed him a full glass of ice water. "Yeah, Rob's coming next week. It's gonna be a blast."

"Cool." Finley took a big swig of water. "So, what've you been up to lately?"

"Not much. I've been hanging around the arcade a bunch and got the high score on tons of games. Including *Donkey Kong* and *Frogger*."

"I didn't think you liked *Frogger* anymore."

"I don't, but I'm the best at it. No one can beat my scores. What have you been up to?"

Finley paused for a moment, lost in thought. Bryce was his best guy friend but he was prone to bragging and over exaggerating his own accomplishments. He had a tendency to become disinterested if someone else talked about the cool things they were up to. Bryce wasn't a bad friend but sometimes he was too wrapped up in his own world to let others share in a moment of glory.

I can't tell him about the summer list. He'll probably think it's dumb and make fun of me and Leah. Besides, we made a promise not to tell anyone. Quickly, Finley thought up a convincing answer and tried to sound casual. "Not much, just hanging around the usual summer places. You know, beach, theater, around the house…"

"Have you seen Leah at all?"

"We're best friends and she lives close by. Of course I've seen her."

Bryce looked vaguely bored and suddenly said, "Oh, you gotta check this out."

Finley followed him to the living room and noticed an orange L-shaped device on the floor. He realized it was a plastic gun with a wire connecting it to a game console. "No way," he exclaimed. "You have *Duck Hunt*? The *Duck Hunt* video game?"

"My folks found it at a garage sale. Wanna play?" Bryce asked, holding up the controller.

Finn scoffed. "Dude, you may as well be asking me if I want pizza. The answer's always 'yes'."

They took turns using the controller as they played. Finley tried shooting at the birds that flew across the screen but he wasn't used to aiming directly at the TV. In the end, he didn't even come close to beating Bryce but he still had tons of fun.

"I keep hitting that stupid, laughing dog in the bonus round."

"You know you're supposed to just hit the birds, right?" Bryce teased.

Finley's stomach growled loudly as Bryce completed his turn. "Do you think we could grab some food once you finish beating me again?"

"Sure, bud. I know a great spot."

About four blocks south of his house was the arcade. Attached to it was a little pizza shop.

"They've got the biggest, cheesiest slices around." Bryce smiled. "Trust me, I know my city."

"I didn't bring any cash." Finn hesitated at the door.

"No worries. I got enough for us both. How about afterwards we hit the arcade? I've got a ton of coins left and then I can show you my high scores?"

"Sure."

Two familiar faces greeted them as they entered the pizza shop.

"Hey guys." Joy beamed.

Dawn waved as she munched on her food.

"Hi, Joy. Hey, Dawn," Finley replied.

"Hey. What's up?" Bryce replied. "What are you guys doing here?"

"My mom's running a bunch of errands today and dropped us off," Dawn explained. "We're going to the mall after this."

"Actually, isn't that her now?" Joy pointed to a woman waving at them through the window.

"We'd better get going," Dawn said, wrapping up the rest of her pizza in a napkin.

"I guess we'll see you at school," Finley said.

"Bye." Joy and Dawn said in unison, as they left.

"That was random." Finley chuckled.

"Did you see the way Dawn was looking at me?" Bryce grinned. "She's so in love with me."

"As if." Finley laughed.

"I'm serious, man. She'd probably marry me if we were old enough and Joy's interested in me, too. I know it."

Finley rolled his eyes and ordered their pizza. Four slices later, they wiped their greasy hands on their shorts and entered the arcade. It was full of colors, flashing lights and loud music.

"Hello, Bryce." One of the attendants waved.

"Hey."

"Going to make any new records today?"

Bryce chuckled. "We'll see." He guided Finn to *Donkey Kong*. "I've got the top score on this one." He pointed to the screen.

Finn read the top score name. "You're A,R?"

Bryce's proud expression faltered and he looked down. "What? They beat me again?"

"Oh, there's yours." Finley pointed to the number two name. "You're BRY, right?"

"Yeah, of course."

Finley smirked at his friend's irritation. "Who's A,R?"

"I don't know," Bryce huffed. "Some wimpy guy that's been beating my high scores all summer. Look, there's their name in third and sixth place. Mine's in fourth and fifth."

Finley examined the screen. "You've never met them?"

"He's become my arch nemesis. He keeps beating me. Then I beat him. Then he beats me. Then I beat him and now I'm gonna do it again." He dug in his pocket for a coin.

"Wait." Finley grabbed his arm. "How long is this going to take? I don't want to watch you play for hours."

Bryce exhaled slowly and calmed down. "You're right. I'll have to beat him another day. We're here to hang out and have fun."

"Hey, *Mario Bros.*" Finley pointed, glad for the distraction. "Look, no one's playing it now. Let's go."

They made their way along the arcade, playing all their favorite two-player games. Bryce won most of them but Finn managed to beat him twice. They were so consumed by their friendly competitions, they weren't aware of how much time had passed until they noticed a mother dragging her daughter out the door.

She cried loudly. "No, I don't wanna go."

"It's almost 5 o'clock." The mother grunted as she pulled her daughter to her feet. "I need to get dinner ready."

"It's almost five?" Finley looked at Bryce, startled by the realization. "I should probably bounce."

Bryce frowned. "But it's so early. Do you have to go now?"

"I'm kinda gamed out anyway."

"All right, we can chill at my place then."

"I have to bike home," Finley argued, "and it takes a while."

Bryce shoved his hands in his pockets. "One of my parents could give you a ride after they're home from work."

"Could they fit my bike in their car trunk?"

"Hmm…probably not. OK, I guess we better bounce."

"Wait." Finley paused. "I didn't get to see your high score on *Frogger* yet."

Bryce smiled. "That's what I'm talking about. It's over here." He led the way and handed Finley a coin. "Fate must be with us because this is my last one. Do me proud."

Finn focused on the screen and slipped the coin in the slot. He moved the frog and darted away from the vehicles.

"Yeah, yeah," Bryce shouted in his ear.

Finley remained silent, concentration practically pouring from his fingertips.

"Go." Bryce chanted, "Go, go, go—no."

The frog was squashed.

"Wow." Finley's shoulders drooped. "That's probably the worst score this game ever got. Zero?"

"You've got more lives left," Bryce reminded him, while trying to hold back his laughter.

"Nah, what's the point in trying anymore?"

Bryce's laugh escaped and he slapped his friend's back. "You died in, like, seven seconds.

Maybe I was wrong and fate's taking a nap or you're just really, really bad at this game."

"There's your name." Finn pointed to the high score. "Proving this is another game you're better at."

Bryce raised his hands in the air. "I told you I'm the best."

"Yeah, yeah, don't rub it in my face," Finn teased. "You know I'd be here every day if I lived closer."

"Nah, dude. You wouldn't have enough cash to last two days, let alone every day. Remember, you just lost after five seconds."

Finn laughed. "Hey, give me some credit. It was at least seven."

"Whatever." Bryce laughed along. "The point is, you use a new coin after you lose a game. In one day, if you lost a game every seven seconds, that's…I don't know how much money you'd lose but I know it's a lot."

"I think I'd better go before we start doing math problems. Save the homework for fall, Bryce. Bye."

"Later, dude."

Finley hopped onto his bike and waved goodbye. He got home just in time to plop down in a chair as his mom was setting the table for dinner. His legs felt rubbery but he didn't regret one moment of the day. It had been great.

20

It was the first rainy day since the Harris family had arrived at the cabin. Leah opened her bedroom window and breathed in the sweet air. It smelled of wet dirt, rich grass and clean rain.

She smiled to herself. *The rain sounds different in the country. It's a deeper and richer sound. If I listen hard enough, I can hear the trees drinking up the water and the bugs skittering for shelter...maybe I'll write a story about this place someday.*

She put her book away, suddenly restless. They had three days left at the cabin and she hadn't done any crafting yet. Earlier that week, she'd decided to make a necklace for Finley with the shells they'd found at the beach. She missed her friend and wanted to surprise him with it so she grabbed her box of art supplies and settled everything down on the table outside. With the porch overhang, she could enjoy the sounds and smell of the rain without getting wet. It was the perfect place to work on her craft, other than the open living room window which inadvertently let her eavesdrop on her parents.

"You've been so happy lately," her mom said.

"I can breathe again, Grace," her dad replied. "No one's pushing deadlines in my face or adding to my pile of paperwork. A huge part of me doesn't want to go back."

"I know," she said.

He chuckled. "Just yesterday I was thinking about how we met."

"Oh no," she teased. "Not this again."

"You were so focused on doing a good job, building that house for Homes for All Souls. You barely noticed me."

Leah's mind raced with a sudden remembrance of her dad explaining how he'd met her mom. *We met at university but didn't connect much until we both signed up to volunteer with Homes for All Souls. Your mom wanted some extra volunteer hours for school credit and Grandpa made me sign up, saying "You'll build character for yourself and homes for others."*

Her mom's voice cut through her thoughts. "Oh, I noticed you Steve…I noticed you were busy sulking the whole time. You were so angry at your father for making you volunteer and to do manual labour, no less."

"But he was right. It built my character."

"Mmm-hmm."

He continued, "I began to see all the little things my parents did for me. All the things I used to take for granted. I appreciated them so much more."

"Do you miss them?"

"Yeah."

She sighed. "It's a shame they live so far away."

"But I also miss the passion I used to have. I loved working with my hands but even more so, I loved helping others in need."

"And you fell in love with me."

He laughed and gave her a hug. Finally, he said, "Staying here, spending time with you and the girls...I feel as though a weight has been lifted. All the worry and dread is off my shoulders and I've been thinking about our future."

"What do you want to do, Steven?"

He hesitated. "I want to quit my job and work for a non-profit organization but, this time, in the office. I have years of financial experience and I think I can navigate through the challenges of fundraising and budgeting."

"Have you prayed about this already?"

"I have. I feel led to do this, Grace. What do you think?"

It was so quiet, Leah thought she hadn't heard the answer or figured her mom had left the room. She was tempted to look through the window but didn't want to give herself away. She'd given up hope of hearing a resolution when suddenly her mom's voice broke the silence.

"I think you're right," she said softly. "You have an incredible understanding of finance and a heart to serve others. You'll likely make less money but with God's blessing, we'll be fine. I'll pray about it, of course."

"Of course," he repeated.

"We'll take it one step at a time."

They were quiet after that. Leah tried concentrating on her project again. She grabbed her hot glue gun and attached a piece of teal beach glass to the string on her necklace. She'd never heard her parents talk about something so serious before. *A new job could change a ton of stuff in our lives. What if Dad doesn't make a lot of money anymore? Would we have to move? Or sell a bunch of our stuff to pay the bills? And what about Finn? If we move, I might have to start high school somewhere else, without my best friend.*

A glob of hot glue slipped from the glass and burned her finger. She cried out in pain and dashed inside to grab a cube of ice from the freezer.

"What's wrong?" her father asked, from the kitchen entrance.

"I burned myself with my hot glue gun," she explained, pressing the ice against her wound.

"Ouch. Want an extra hand?"

"Sure," she said, examining her finger. It was red but thankfully didn't have a blister.

She joined her father on the porch and regarded the messy table.

"Now I understand why there's an extension cord out here." He smiled and examined the glue gun.

Uh-oh. Does that mean he figured out I could hear his conversation with Mom? She changed the subject and asked, "Do you know how to poke holes through shells?"

"No," he said, lowering the glue gun. "Leah, where did you find this beach glass? It's quite beautiful."

"On the beach, with Finley—" She stopped herself before saying more about their secret summer list.

"I've never seen any there," he pondered. "I seem to have missed a lot of things, lately."

She tried to make him feel better. "I mean, it was kinda hard to find. A lot of people must have missed it."

"Yes…"

"I wanted to make a necklace with these shells," she said, mindlessly picking one up then putting it back down.

"You should probably clean them first," he suggested. "And the library may have some books on shell jewelery."

"That's a good idea," she mused. "OK, I can work on this more after we get home." She piled her stuff back into the box but left the glue gun to cool. "Thanks for your help, Dad."

She left quickly, feeling uncomfortable that she'd eavesdropped; especially because her dad may have figured out what she'd done. She spent the rest of the day reading in her room and gazing at the magical trees in the backyard. They helped her find solace from her guilty conscience and uncertainty about the future.

She got up late the next day, weary from sleeping poorly. She kept dreaming her family moved to a strange, new neighborhood and no one wanted to be her friend. By the time she entered the kitchen, her whole family was sitting around the table, sipping coffee.

"Good morning," her mother said, with a smile.

Her dad looked at his watch. "You slept in pretty late this morning."

"Yeah." Diane looked her up and down. "When's the last time you slept longer than me?"

"I didn't sleep well." Leah sat down.

Diane got up from her seat. "If anyone needs me, I'll be reading outside."

"Actually…" Her mother rested a hand on Diane's arm. "Your father and I want to discuss something with you girls."

Leah's stomach sank. *Is this it? Are they going to say we're moving?*

"Your father and I have been talking and praying a lot lately," her mom continued, "and this concerns the whole family so we decided not to prolong sharing the news. Do you want to tell them, Steven?"

He looked at his wife then back at his daughters. "I'm quitting my job."

Leah stared silently.

"You're quitting?" Diane asked.

"Yes." He held his wife's hand.

Mrs. Harris explained, "We believe his job has become unhealthy—"

"Wait." Diane interrupted, "You're not sick, are you?"

"Not physically," he explained. "Your mother means it has become mentally and emotionally unhealthy for me. Upper management has unrealistic expectations of our work ethic."

"We've all noticed a change in your father since his business has undergone new management," their mom added.

"Yes," Leah said, softly.

She suddenly realized how selfish she'd been. *I didn't want him to get a new job because I was scared of moving...but he's given up so much to provide for our family. He's missed out on family events because he's been so exhausted. How long has he been unhappy? Last month he yelled at Diane, out of impatience. He never did that before.* She looked at him with a critical eye. *Has he lost weight? His cheekbones and jaw line seem sharper; but there's a new sparkle in his eye and yesterday I heard him humming a song. When was the last time I heard that?*

Diane asked, "What does that mean for us?"

Leah steadied herself and said, "I'm willing to move if it means you'll get a good job and be happy again, Dad."

His eyes sparkled even more. "Thank you, my dear daughter."

Her mother gently squeezed Diane's shoulder. "But we don't plan on moving."

Their dad shook his head. "No. Diane, you only have two years left of school. Moving could jeopardize your grades and hurt your chances of going to a good college. Leah, you need a good start at high school. We've got a loving community in our neighborhood and church that supports you girls in a way we can't as your parents."

Leah was so relieved; she had to blink hard to stop herself from tearing up.

"We're going to look for something available in the area," their mother said.

"And if I don't find exactly what I'm looking for, I'll find a compromise," their father said.

"What are you looking for, Dad?" Diane asked.

"I plan to still work in finance but for a non-profit organization. I want to serve others that need a little extra help."

"The way you did with Homes for All Souls," Leah offered.

"Exactly." Her mom smiled.

"Will anything change for us?" Diane asked.

"Perhaps financially," he said, in a matter-of-fact tone, "but nothing drastic."

Diane looked reassured.

Leah rubbed his back. "I'm glad you're quitting, Dad. You've definitely been happier since we got here."

"Fresh air does wonders to clear the mind." her mom said, smirking.

"When are you telling your boss you're quitting?" Leah asked.

"I'll give my two weeks' notice on Monday," he said, "and start looking for a new job that evening."

"It's a bit of a risk," their mother reminded. "Normally, it's best to line up a new job before quitting your current one. We may have to live off of our savings for a while."

"It's worth it," Diane said, shrugging, "and if I can help in any way, just let me know."

"Me too." Leah nodded.

"Thank you, girls." Their dad smiled. "You can always keep your eyes open for opportunities but, more importantly, pray that I'll find the place I'm supposed to be."

Diane gave him a 'thumbs up'. "Got it."

Leah gave him a hug. "Always, Dad."

The remainder of their time at the cabin was more family-oriented. All together they hiked to a sight-seeing area overlooking the surrounding valley. By the time they reached the top, they were all out of breath but the view was worth it. They played card games on the porch table in the evening and warmed themselves by the fire at night, as they roasted potatoes in the smoldering ashes. They all agreed it was the best family vacation they'd ever had. As ready as they were to go home at the end of the week, a part of them didn't want it to end.

21

It had been a week since Finley spent the day with Bryce and he was feeling lonely and bored again. There were only so many video games he could play and TV shows to watch before nothing felt entertaining anymore. He grabbed the kitchen phone and punched in Bryce's number again. Even if he had to deal with the heat of the day and the threat of having sore leg muscles tomorrow, he was willing to bike over.

"Hello?" Bryce asked on the other end.

"Hey, it's Finn."

"Hey, dude."

"Are you free to hang out today?"

Bryce inhaled sharply. "Actually, my cousin Rob is here now."

"Oh, yeah? When did he arrive?"

"A couple days ago and guess what? I totally convinced him to go back to the water park."

"How?" Finn asked.

"I told him kids rip their swim trunks all the time. Plus, it happened to him when he was a little kid. He looks so different now, no one will recognize him."

Finley laughed.

"Yesterday we dominated the pool, it was awesome. Hey, we're going again in about ten minutes. Do you wanna come with us?"

"In ten minutes? I can't bike to your house in time and I don't have a different way to get there."

"Bummer. Your house is in the opposite direction we're headed, otherwise…"

"It's all right, dude. Have fun with Rob and make sure to tell me if he does anything funny this time."

"Sure thing. Later."

Finley sighed and walked aimlessly around the house. It was too hot to do anything outside, there was no one to play a board game with in the living room and he didn't want to clean his bedroom. There was nothing to do. It was days, such as this, when he disliked being an only child. By the time he meandered to the basement, he was so dissatisfied with everything he flopped onto the couch and just stared at the ceiling. He'd unintentionally fallen asleep and was startled awake when he heard his father calling his name from the stairs.

"Finley? What are you doing?"

Finley stretched and got to his feet. "Nothing. Is it already past five?"

"Yes. What do you mean you were doing nothing?"

He shrugged. "It's kinda boring here by myself."

"Your throne still needs to be properly sealed to withstand the weather. Would you like to work on that together?"

"Nah, that's OK. It's more yours and Leah's project anyway."

His dad looked at him silently. After a moment, he motioned for Finley to follow him and led him to their backyard. Together, they looked at the throne.

He asked, "What do you think of this throne, Finley?"

He shuffled his bare feet on the grass. "I don't know. It looks cool."

"This is how I hopped your throne would look," his dad said. "I was so excited when you announced you were going to build something. I thought you were learning to be responsible by taking the initiative, working hard on a project and seeing it through to its completion. That's why I didn't help you and Leah at first."

Finley avoided his father's eyes. "I wanted to make something by myself."

"Why?"

"Because, I—I—" Finley stumbled over his words. The frustration and embarrassment he felt after Leah and his dad had destroyed his throne were coming back. Finally, the words he hadn't admitted to anyone spilled out. "I wanted to prove I could do it by myself. I didn't need your help, I could do it alone. I'm older. I'm mature. I wanted to prove that to both of us."

"That's what I wanted, too. Finley, I wanted you to succeed."

"But you and Leah tore apart my throne then you replaced what I built with something much better. It was as though you were saying it wasn't good enough...*I* wasn't good enough."

"Hey." Mr. Davidson's voice grew so loud, it shocked Finley into looking at him. "Never believe that, Finley. You've always been more than good enough. Don't ever underestimate your worth. I love you more than I ever thought I could love someone."

Finley looked back at the ground, too emotional to keep his father's gaze.

His dad calmed down. "If your self-esteem depends on the things you accomplish, you're sure to fall apart, sooner or later. Everybody makes mistakes. That's where love and grace come in. You need to love yourself and understand your family will never stop loving you."

He patted his son's back and they silently stood together for a long time. Mrs. Davidson waved to her husband from the kitchen window, signaling that dinner was ready. He signaled back he and Finley would eat later. When he felt his son's breathing slow down, he removed his hand.

"Sit with me for a moment," he invited.

They sat across from one another on the soft ground and mindlessly picked at the blades of grass as they talked.

"Finley, the reason why I helped Leah remake the throne was because I wanted you both to learn from it. What have you done during these past two weeks?"

Finn shrugged. "I dunno. Played video games, watched TV and I hung out with Bryce, once."

His dad dropped his blade of grass. "That's my point. Right there."

Finn looked up at his dad in confusion.

"Leah was willing to put in a lot of hard work to get a good final result. You tried but at the end of the day, you were satisfied with a low-quality project."

"I worked hard, too," Finn argued.

"But you didn't prepare. You didn't make a blueprint or take time to work out the small details. You didn't take advantage of all your resources, you didn't come to me for advice or do any research at the library. Quality work comes from knowledge, experience and a lot of help and guidance."

"I just wanted to have fun," Finley explained.

His dad continued, "And that's not a bad thing but you underestimated the benefits of making a plan and following through. If having fun is your only goal in life, you're not always going to have a good result. You're entering high school in the fall. You can't cram all your studying into one night before your final exams because there's more material you need to remember. There needs to be preparation. You need to study days in advance—"

Finley interrupted, "So this lesson you wanted to teach me was about studying?"

"It's about life," his father corrected him then joked, "life doesn't give anything for free except air, sunshine and death. People need to work hard if they want something and a strong work ethic can go a long way."

Finn asked, "Is that why you're making me get a job next summer?"

His father answered, "Partially, and so you can understand the value of money better. Why do you think your mother and I have jobs?"

"To pay the bills."

"Exactly. We're fortunate to have a good home, two vehicles, clothes, food…you get the idea. It's a lot of work to keep up the lifestyle we live and it doesn't just require having jobs, it also involves household chores. Mowing the lawn, cooking meals, cleaning the house, all these need to be done in addition to our work schedule." He pointed to the throne. "This project is a symbol of hard work leading to a reward. Leah understood that quickly and was willing to put in the extra hours. I'd hoped you'd figure it out and join us."

Finley looked from the chair to his dad. "Oh."

"I believe it's time for you to help out more around the house. Your mother and I would appreciate it. You're not a child anymore; you're old enough to be a part of Team Davidson."

Finley smirked at the name but didn't dare tell his father how goofy it sounded. Instead, he asked, "How can I help?"

"I want you to decide," his father said, "but I'd like you to choose at least two chores to do on a regular basis and nothing simple. Don't just take the garbage to the curb."

"I won't do that," Finley reassured.

"Of course, there are perks to being on our team." His father winked. "You can borrow our equipment for free. For instance, you may use our lawnmower to mow the neighbors' yards for some extra cash. Your bedtime will be later; you can help plan meals...but limit the chicken nuggets and fries to just one meal a week."

Finley chuckled. "Don't worry. There's also pizza and burgers and Mom's cheesy casserole I can suggest."

His dad laughed along. "There is freedom and responsibility with growing up. As you become older, you'll learn that more and more." He paused, a cheeky grin spread on his face. "And, if you continue with planning those kinds of meals, you may learn the responsibility of taking heartburn medication earlier than expected."

Finn's smile grew larger. "OK, OK. Message received. So, will you tell me how to spend my money when I have a job?"

"I'd be more than willing to give you some advice," his father answered.

"What about a car? Could I buy one when I'm sixteen?"

Mr. Davidson laughed again. "Yes but only if you buy a reliable car and can pay to maintain it."

Finley nodded in approval. "Cool."

"Responsibility has its moments of greatness," his dad assured.

"I'm sorry about the throne. I bet you and Leah had a lot of fun building it."

"Yes, we did."

"Could we...finish it, Dad?"

"You mean seal the wood?"

"Yeah and paint it or something? I have an idea on the color."

Mr. Davidson smiled. "We can pick some up after dinner."

During the rest of the week, Finley kept his eyes out for different chores he could do around the house. One evening, he saw his mom resting with her feet up and wondered how it felt to stand on them for eight hours straight. He decided he'd help her by setting the table and cleaning up after all their meals. To help his dad, he decided to mow the lawn every Thursday. That was when his Dad's favorite TV show was on and because Finley didn't like the show himself, he'd spend the time doing something useful. He even decided to put up a couple posters nearby, advertising he'd cut other people's lawns for a small price. The more he thought about owning a car at sixteen, the more excited he was to start working. He figured, in autumn, he could advertise raking leaves and in winter he could shovel snow, although his dad cautioned that schoolwork should come first. On Saturday, Finley and his dad worked on staining the throne. He'd picked out a cherry color, which beautifully accentuated the wood grain and glistened in the sunlight.

"This a wonderful choice in color," his dad said, as they rubbed off the excess liquid with a rag.

A fruit fly landed on the throne and got stuck in the wet stain. Finley carefully picked it off.

"Yeah," he agreed. "I thought it would look great with the green grass and leaves."

Mr. Davidson stepped back from the area he was working on. "It looks more regal now."

Finn nodded vigorously. At first, when his father told him to do more chores, he hadn't been eager about it but he understood the reasoning behind his dad's decision. Over the past couple days; his attitude had progressed into one of enjoyment. He wasn't irritable and bored all the time because he had something productive to do and it felt good to help others. His mother would often sit at the table and chat with him while he did the dishes. He was making bigger and better plans for the throne with his father, too. Plus, he already had two people call about his lawn mowing advertisement. He arranged to do them in the late afternoon so he could keep his work schedule the same once school started.

Mr. Davidson looked proudly at Finley as they worked on the throne. He was sure his son's enthusiasm toward work would diminish over time but he'd enjoy it as long as it lasted.

He asked, "Did I ever tell you about the time I was fishing with your grandfather and I almost pierced my ear?"

Finley looked at him with wide eyes. "What? No."

Mr. Davidson laughed. "I was about ten or eleven years old when we went fishing at a nearby lake. It had been a dry year so the lake was emptier than usual and we were having a hard time finding a good spot from which to fish. Anyway, I was following your grandfather along the shore and it was muddy, normally that part of the lake would be underwater, and my foot got stuck in the mud. It was deep, too. The mud went almost to my knee. I tried to pull myself free but lost my balance and almost landed on my face."

Finley snickered at the idea of his father's face being caked in mud.

"Oh, it gets better." His dad chuckled. "I managed to fall on my hands but, in doing so, I let go of my fishing rod. It stuck straight up in the mud a little ways from me. So…there I was, feet and hands stuck in the mud, my butt wagging in the air and this whole time Dad's still walking ahead of me, completely unaware."

Finley smiled. "Didn't you yell for help?"

His dad nodded. "You bet I yelled. Dad turned around and I'll never forget his face. At first he was surprised and looked as if he were going to laugh but stopped when he saw my fishing rod. Then he got angry. Those things aren't cheap."

Finn asked, "What did he do?"

"He put his stuff down then came and got my fishing rod. He said he didn't want me to step on it. He put it with his own stuff then came back and helped pull me up. I was a mess and wanted to go home but Dad was practical, gave me back my fishing rod and told me to rinse everything off in the lake. I obeyed him without complaining. Sure, the water was cold but, at the end of the day, I wasn't about to sit in his truck with mud all over me. So, I took off my boots and washed my feet. Then I washed my boots, hands and rod. Dad was waiting for me on the shore and, as I was walking back, what do you know, my foot got stuck again. The same one too and, once again, I was about to land on my face."

Finley laughed. "No."

"Oh yeah, however, this time I had learned my lesson. I tried to save my fishing rod so I tossed it over to my father, where the ground was drier but I was in a hurry and accidentally tossed it poorly. As it spun in the air, the hook flew in the air and caught on my ear. See?" He showed a scar on the top of his left ear.

Finley peered at it. "That's from a fishing hook? Cool."

"It didn't feel cool." His dad laughed. "The hook was tightly latched onto my ear and it stopped my fishing rod in its tracks. Of course, it landed in the mud again. Then I fell in the mud and, while my dad was trying to pull the hook from my ear, which took a while because it was barbed, he also got stuck in the mud. Needless to say, we didn't go fishing that day. We went straight to the hospital, I got three stitches then we went home for a bath."

"Was Grandpa angry?"

"For a little while; but, after we were cleaned up, I heard him talking to your grandmother about our day and they were both laughing. I must have been a pretty miserable looking kid, knee-deep in the mud, with a fishing hook stuck in my ear."

Finley cackled. "I can't believe I never heard this story before."

Mr. Davidson chuckled. "Yep. It was one of the best and worst days of my life."

"What made you think of it now?"

"Huh…" His dad mulled it over. "I guess because fishing was our special thing to do together. In the same way this throne is yours and mine."

"Thanks for all your help, Dad. I'm super excited to see it when we finish everything. It's gonna be so much better than I imagined."

"You're welcome, Finley. Tomorrow, when this has dried completely, we'll do that last step we talked about."

"Leah's going to be so excited when she sees it."

22

"Are you serious?" Leah asked Finley, as she looked at the throne.

Her family had returned home yesterday and spent the day unpacking everything from their trip. Finley had called after dinner, asking if she wanted to stop by but she was exhausted so she decided to come by the next morning, instead.

"Wanna hop on?" Finley asked.

"Duh."

He held it steady as she sat on the throne then gave her a push. Yesterday he and his dad had added the eye bolts and rope then hung it from the tree in their backyard. Now they had a swinging throne next to the tree house.

Suddenly, Leah's smile faded and she stopped swinging. "Hey, Finn…I'm sorry about working with your dad—"

He interrupted, "You don't have to be sorry; you didn't do anything wrong. I should apologize to you; I was going through some stuff and it wasn't fair for me to put the blame on you."

"Oh," she nodded slowly. "Are…you OK now? Do you want to talk about it?"

"Nah, it's fine. Dad and I worked it out."

"Are we OK?"

He smiled. "We are. That is, if you forgive me for how I treated you."

She returned his smile. "You're forgiven."

"Thanks."

She began pumping her legs again. "This is so cool and the color you chose to paint it is great."

"It's actually stain," he corrected. "Dad taught me the difference."

"Well, whatever it is, it looks great."

"How was your trip?" Finley asked.

"Fantastic." She beamed and soared higher. "We went on hikes, used the fire pit a ton, played card games practically every evening and just hung out."

She left out the part about her dad planning to quit his job. He asked the whole family to keep this information a secret until he gave his official notice at work and she was going to keep her promise.

She pumped her legs and asked, "What about you? What did you do while I was gone?"

Finley's eyes went up and down as he watched her. "Well, you already know about the work

Dad and I did together. And…what else did I do…? Oh, I hung out with Bryce one day. We stopped by a pizza place and saw Joy and Dawn. Then we went to the arcade and he beat me at almost every game." He laughed. "Other than that, I didn't do much."

"Sounds relaxing," she commented.

"Nah, it was pretty boring but now I've got a couple jobs lined up to cut grass. I'm gonna make a little cash and save up for a car."

She skidded to a stop. "You're getting a car?"

He smirked. "Not for a while. It'll take a lot of work to save up for one."

"That's so cool."

"Tomorrow afternoon is my first day. I want to have it finished before my customer gets home from work."

"Are you nervous?" she asked.

"Nah. I've cut grass tons of times. It's no big deal," he replied but secretly he was a little excited. "Dad said I can use our lawnmower."

"I thought you didn't want a job." Leah raised an eyebrow. "That's why we're doing our summer list this year."

He shrugged. "It's just a little job. I've only got three yards to mow, besides this one," he said, motioning to the backyard, "and we can still finish our list."

"Wanna do one today? It's been forever since we've hung out. What was the last thing we did—" She stopped, suddenly remembering the embarrassment she felt from watching the R-rated movie.

Finley quickly spoke up, trying to move past the awkward reminder. "Let's look for a new world today. We'll definitely find a cool, new place around here."

"I know about a diner," Leah suggested. "It'll be a new place for you."

"You've been there?"

"Yeah, Diane took me earlier this summer."

He thought about it then decided against it. "Nah. It should be new for both of us. Besides, does a restaurant qualify as a new world?"

"I dunno. I thought world meant place."

"Yeah, that makes sense but, to me, a world is bigger than a diner."

"A mall?"

"Maybe." He rubbed his chin. "Yeah, that could work or a park or something."

"We could ride around on our bikes and look for something new."

"OK, I'll get my bike and meet you at your house," Finley said.

"I'm gonna quickly make a sandwich to take along," Leah said. "Who knows how long this'll take."

"Good idea, I'll do the same. See you in a bit."

In ten minutes, they were on their bikes, riding around the city. The cloudy sky made the air cooler than normal. It was perfect weather for riding a bike all day. They rode through a couple quiet neighborhoods then quickly decided they had nothing interesting to offer. They mostly consisted of houses with an occasional school or small park popping up—nothing big enough to be considered a new world.

"This is boring," Leah said as they rode down another quiet street.

"Maybe we should explore the busier streets?" Finley suggested.

"The ones closer to the middle of the city?"

"Yeah. There's tons of stuff there."

"Isn't that a little too far to bike?"

"I biked to Bryce's house in less than an hour," he reassured. "Although, I went pretty fast and my legs were a little sore the next day."

"That's not too bad," Leah said, "but let's stop somewhere for lunch first. I'm getting hungry."

"Already?"

She explained, "I didn't have breakfast today because I was so excited to come over to your place."

He laughed. "OK, OK. Maybe we'll find another small park around here."

Eventually, they found one tucked behind a group of houses. They rested under a large maple tree and ate contentedly. A couple of young kids were playing on the slides.

"How do kids do that?" Finley said between bites.

Leah looked over. "What?"

"Do the same thing over and over again, without getting tired. Each time they go down the slide, they laugh as though it's the greatest thing in the world."

"Well, I can't talk." Leah smirked. "I was swinging in your backyard this morning."

"They just go up and down, up and down." Finley continued watching them.

"We used to do that," Leah reminded.

"I guess."

"And we made up stories. Do you remember the one about a snake chasing us on the ground so we had to climb up on the ladder and when we got to the top, we had to slide down so a dragon didn't breathe fire on us."

"A dragon? I thought an eagle tried to grab us with her talons and feed us to her babies."

Leah laughed. "I think we had a couple different versions of the story."

Finley continued to watch the kids. "We had such a great imagination back then."

She argued, "We still do. We're finishing our summer wish list, aren't we?"

"Yeah but I mean, we don't make up stories and play them out anymore."

"Um…do you want to?"

He shook his head. "No. No, of course not. It's not the same anymore. It isn't as fun as it used to be."

"We're growing up, Finn. Soon you'll have a moustache."

He looked at her and saw she was covering her mouth to stop from laughing. He retorted, "Well then, soon you'll have a full-time job."

"You're having six kids."

"And you're having ten."

She laughed. "You're going to retire."

He yelled. "You're going to spend winters knitting sweaters for your grandkids."

"Fine then, I'll make one for you, too."

"Thank you very much. I'd like a blue one, please."

They were laughing so hard, the kids stopped playing and stared at them.

In the afternoon, they biked around the center of the city. They passed by a few places they hadn't been in, such as thrift stores, vehicle repair shops and boutiques but nothing that fit their description of a world.

"Hey." Leah mentioned, "A sign back there pointed to an art gallery. Wanna go?"

"Nah."

A little while later they found a museum.

"Maybe we'll find something there?" Finley suggested.

She disliked the idea. "It's a pioneer museum. We don't want to look at an old world. We want a new one."

"I'm running out of ideas," he admitted.

"Too bad we don't have a space themed museum. Or that place... What's it called? Where you sit in a chair and the ceiling shows a bunch of stars and someone talks about them..."

"A planetarium. Yeah, it would be perfect for this summer task."

Leah replied, "Exactly, or an underground cafe no one knows about; a secret place just for us."

"I don't think we'll find one in the city," Finley said.

"A hidden gem. That's what we want. Kinda similar to the beach, where we found our treasure. Somewhere no one goes."

"Please don't tell me you wanna bike all the way to the beach," he whined. "I'm already getting tired."

She reassured him. "No, not there. We need someplace new. Maybe we should stop biking today and come up with some more ideas for tomorrow."

"Sounds good to me.

"Before we go home, let's make a pit stop."

"Where?"

Leah grinned. "Just follow me."

She led the way to the little diner Diane took her to a few weeks ago.

"Dee's Diner? Is this the place you were talking about earlier?" Finley asked, as he got off his bike.

"Yeah, isn't it great? She said practically no one knows about it except high school kids. This is sorta their secret hide out."

"It's pretty cool," he said, taking in the decor, "but I thought we agreed it doesn't count as a new world."

She smiled. "We did but I was craving one of their chocolate milkshakes. They're so yummy. Want one? My treat."

He smiled back. "Definitely."

They ordered their drinks to go then biked the rest of the way home.

"I'll try to think of another place where we can look," Finley said, as they reached Leah's house.

"Same here. Meet you tomorrow at ten?"

"Yep, and thanks for the milkshake. You were right, it's delicious."

"Welcome to the perks of almost being in high school." She winked.

23

As agreed, they met the next morning. The sun was out, promising to make the day a hot one.

"Hey," Leah said, as she met Finn at the sidewalk.

"Hey. How are your legs today?"

"A little sore," she admitted, "but once we start biking, the muscles will warm up and feel better."

"Did you know our bodies have over six hundred muscles?"

"No."

"The largest one is the gluteus maximus, *aka*, our butts," he said, laughing.

Leah didn't find it nearly as funny. "Anyway…how are your muscles feeling today?"

Finley rubbed his left leg. "Mine are sore and stiff."

"Would you rather wait until tomorrow?"

He shook his head. "I'll be all right. As you said, they'll feel better after we bike for a bit."

"Do you have any ideas about where we should look today?"

Again he shook his head. "Not any good ones. How about you?"

She unconsciously scratched at a mosquito bite on her arm. "Actually, yes. I think we've been looking in all the wrong places."

"Duh."

She rolled her eyes. "I mean, we've been looking in the city when we need to be looking in the opposite direction. We should get away from the buildings and the people and look in the woods, just west of here."

"You want to go into the woods?" he asked, incredulously.

"Yeah."

"We could get lost."

"We don't have to go far in. There's a highway right beside it. We can keep it in sight the whole time and, because today's sunny, we'll always know which way is south."

"Why?"

"Because in the middle of the day, you face south and the sun at the same time."

"Oh, of course. Yeah, I knew that."

She raised an eyebrow and said sarcastically, "Uh-huh, sure you did, Mr. Facts-Sharing-Guy. Anyway, what do you think?"

He shrugged. "We haven't found anything yet. Maybe you're right. We need to try something totally different." He held out a finger as a warning. "As long as we don't get lost."

Leah smiled and brought out a piece of chalk from her small backpack. "To be extra careful, we can mark each tree we pass so we can retrace our steps later."

"You thought of everything," he marvelled.

"Mom showed me a trick or two while we were hiking last week."

"Well then, lead the way."

They biked slower, still tired from yesterday's riding, until gradually their muscles didn't hurt anymore. It took an hour to exit the city limits but, soon after they reached the woods Leah was talking about. They stopped on the outskirts and laid down their bikes.

"I don't know if we should ride in there," Leah cautioned.

Finn agreed, "Yeah, I don't want to pop my tires on any of the fallen sticks or rocks or whatever's hidden under the leaves."

There was a layer of foliage scattered on the ground but it wasn't enough to hide the uneven ground.

"Now what?" he asked.

"I hadn't thought about it," Leah admitted. "Should we bring our bikes with us or hide them in the trees? I don't want anyone to steal them."

"There are some bushes over there." Finn pointed. "We could hide them on the other side so no one can see them but us."

"Perfect."

The air was heavier among the trees. More humid, too, and it smelled of moss and dirt. As they walked, the fallen leaves softened the ground and silenced their steps.

"It's so quiet," Finley whispered. "Other than the highway, I can't hear anything."

"I like it." Leah smiled. "It's not as peaceful as the trails by the cabin but it's still nice."

She marked the bark of the trees with her piece of chalk as they walked deeper into the woods.

"Hey," Finley asked, "do you want to know something cool?

Leah smirked knowingly. "Uh-oh. Here we go with another fact. What is it this time?"

"There's a type of tree that grows in tropical forests and it's got super colorful layers of bark. Red, blue, purple, green—"

"Are you serious? It's that colorful?"

"It's called rainbow eucalyptus, I think. It sheds its bark and when the layer underneath mixes with air, it turns into all sorts of colors."

"That's so cool. Describe it more so I can picture it in my head."

He paused in thought. "OK. You know when you have a piece of paper then dump different colors of paint on the top?"

"Yeah."

"Then you hold up the paper so the paint runs down? It looks similar to that."

"I wish we had them here. I'd love to draw one."

Finley looked around. "A forest full of those trees would definitely be a new world for us to discover."

Leah regarded the trees surrounding them and noticed the variety of colors they contained on their bark and moss. Brown, grey, white, green, yellow, red. "Yeah, there are lots of colors here but it's not the same."

Silently, they walked deeper into the woods.

"Hmm…I dunno about this place, Leah," Finley said, after several minutes had passed. "There's nothing special to make it a new world."

"You're right." Leah sighed. "I don't know what I was expecting. Of course there's nothing here."

Finn heard the disappointment in her voice and tried to lighten the mood. "To be fair, it has merit. It looks as though no one goes here, which kinda makes it a new, unexplored world."

"True," Leah admitted, "but, if we don't find anything here, where else can we look? I'm seriously doubting we can cross this challenge off our summer list."

"Maybe we'll have to try another time." He shrugged. "After we get our driver's licenses we can take a road trip or something."

Leah contemplated the idea. "That would be fun. We could get a huge map then drive across the country and stop at quaint, little places along the way…or just drive for the day and see where the road takes us."

"Yeah. We've got lots of time to complete this task in the future. If we go—"

"Shh." Leah held up a hand. "Do you hear that?"

Finn listened for a beat. "I hear traffic…?"

"I thought I heard something," Leah said, cocking her head to one side. "Wait until the traffic dies down…There, I heard it again."

He shook his head. "I don't hear anything."

"It's coming from over there." Leah pointed to their left.

"What is it?"

"I don't know. It sounds as though something is hissing."

"What? A snake?"

"No, it's bigger. It's gotta be an engine or something," Leah said and started walking toward the noise.

Finley grabbed her arm. "What are you doing?"

"I want to know what's making that sound."

"Are you nuts? Nothing that hisses is good. Snakes, gas leaks, people laughing between their teeth, it's all bad."

She looked at her friend. "Just a peek, Finn. I won't get close. Come on, aren't you curious?"

He exhaled sharply. He knew if he didn't look, the sound would haunt him forever. He gave in.

"Fine; but we're not going close. If it's an animal or a person, we're running out of here. OK?"

"OK."

They tiptoed toward the sound, pausing every once in a while when they couldn't hear it over the sounds of traffic. As they grew closer, the sound evolved from hissing to babbling. Then to gurgling. Then splashing.

"It's water," Finley remarked, relief shooting along his skin.

"It must be a creek." Leah scanned the area. "I didn't know there was one around here."

"Wait. Is that it?" He pointed to an opening in the trees.

Together they drew near, the sound now undeniably water. They stepped between a couple shrubs and looked at the view in front of them. The area had fewer trees and sunlight trickled through the leaves. Soft, green grass emerged along the edges of the creek and a couple flowers were in bloom.

"Wow." Leah gasped.

"Wait…" Finley said in disbelief, "Did—did we just find a new world?"

Small mushrooms sprouted among the roots of the trees and a squirrel bounded up a trunk when it saw them. Leah felt the same magical quality in the air as she'd felt with the trees behind her aunt and uncle's cabin.

Leah laughed. "I think so." *This is a place where fairies live and frogs waltz along the lily pads and birds sing melodies they learned from the stars during a full moon.*

Finley stuttered, "This is…I mean, I…How did we—"

"It doesn't matter," Leah interrupted. "We don't need answers, let's just enjoy our world."

They meandered onto the grass, breathing in new scents of life and wet earth. They sat together and ate their packed lunches in peace. Shrubbery encased the area, blocking out most of the traffic noise.

"I could make up so many stories about this place," Leah said dreamily.

"I know what you mean." Finley smiled.

"We should come back tomorrow with a pencil and paper."

"Absolutely. Oh, that reminds me, I'm cutting Mr. Welsh's grass this afternoon. How long did it take us to get here?"

Leah shrugged. "An hour on our bikes and maybe another hour of walking; although, we wandered around for a while."

"In that case, I should probably go," he said. "I want to mow his grass before he gets home from work."

"Aren't people usually done work at five? You have lots of time."

"No, Mr. Welsh is a teacher at some private school around here; but, during the summer, he gives private tutoring to kids in the area. He'll be home around three."

"All right." Leah got to her feet. "If you're going then I'm going."

"You can stay, if you want," he offered.

"I don't think it'll be as much fun alone and it's probably not the safest idea anyway. What if I tripped on a rock or tree root and hurt myself?"

He nodded. "I guess you're right. Sorry to make you leave, though."

She smiled. "It's all right. Now that we found this place, we can come back any time."

Finley had just finished cutting Mr. Welsh's lawn when Mr. Welsh arrived home. He wiped his forehead with the back of his arm, suddenly realizing how hot the day had become.

"Hello, Finley." Mr. Welsh approached him. "Done already, are you?"

"Yes, sir. The front and back yard are all done. I wanted to finish before you got home so you wouldn't have to hear the lawnmower."

"That's very considerate of you. How much do I owe you?"

"Five dollars, sir."

"Five dollars?" Mr. Welsh's eyebrows raised. "The last person who mowed my lawn charged ten."

"Perhaps I have less experience," Finley suggested.

"Well, how about we keep my usual rate?" Mr. Welsh smiled and handed him ten dollars. "Let's consider it a bonus for your consideration and getting the job done early."

Finn couldn't stop himself from smiling. *This is turning out to be a fantastic day.* "Thank you, Mr. Welsh," he said graciously. "Do you want me to cut it next week, too?"

"As long as it's not raining, I'd appreciate that."

"Enjoy the rest of your day." Finley waved goodbye and pushed the mower onto the sidewalk.

"And the same to you." Mr. Welsh waved back.

As Finn was walking back to his house, he noticed a lawn with very long grass. Normally, he wouldn't give it much thought but with his new job, he was extra attentive to lawn maintenance.

He read the name on the mailbox. *Mrs. Jody. Don't I know that name? …Yes, she's the nice, old lady Mom sometimes talks to in the grocery store. I think Mom said when she was little, Mrs. Jody used to babysit her. I wonder if she can't manage taking care of her yard anymore.*

He paused, looking at the lawn and feeling extra thankful after the great day he had. With Mr. Welsh paying twice as much as his usual rate, he figured he could afford to be just as generous. Finley started his mower and slowly worked on cutting the grass. It was so long, he had to mow over it twice to get all the extra bits he missed. It also required some extra hard pushing in a couple places but, with all the biking he'd been doing lately, his muscles could take it. Every once in a while, he glanced at the house windows, hoping Mrs. Jody didn't realize what he was doing.

I'm just going to sneak in and sneak out. I don't need the credit for mowing her lawn and I don't want her to pay me. She may not be able to afford it anyway. This is a simple way for me to help someone else.

When he was finished, he slunk back to the sidewalk and scurried home.

"I made it," he said happily to himself, as he pushed the mower into the garage.

After a cool shower and a large glass of water, the phone rang.

His mom answered it. "Hello? Oh yes, it's nice to hear from you. How are you doing? Oh?" She looked at Finn curiously as she listened to the speaker talk for a long while.

He squirmed. *Who's on the phone? Are they talking about me? Did someone see me walking in the woods when I shouldn't be or did Mr. Welsh dislike the quality of the work I did and he's going to fire me?*

Finally, she said, "I couldn't say one way or the other. May I call you back? OK, bye-bye." She hung up the phone and walked over to her son. "That was Mrs. Jody on the phone."

His muscles relaxed slightly and he tried to sound casual. "OK."

"Someone mowed her grass this afternoon but she doesn't know who did it. She remembered seeing your flyer at the grocery store and wants to know if it was you."

"Oh."

Finn wondered if he'd done something wrong. *What if Mrs. Jody hadn't wanted her grass cut? Maybe the grass was special and needed to be long. Or someone else was supposed to cut it and I accidentally took away their job.*

His mom asked, "Did you do it?"

"Um…" He paused. *I don't want Mrs. Jody to think she owes me something but now I'm drawing a blank on a good excuse. Mom will see through it and know I'm not telling her everything.* He took a deep breath and said hesitantly, "I finished mowing Mr. Welsh's yard…and, on my way home, I noticed her grass was long. So I cut it."

"You mowed her lawn?"

"Yes."

"Without her asking you to do it?"

He hung his head. "Yes."

"And without getting paid for it?"

"Yes."

His mom grabbed him by the shoulders and pulled him in for a hug. "Finley, you sweet boy. You helped her and asked for nothing in return."

He pulled away. "I don't want her to pay me, Mom. If she knows I cut her grass, she might—"

She chuckled. "Don't worry, I won't tell her it was you. I'll say it was a good Samaritan who was happy to help."

He sighed in relief. "Thanks, Mom."

She hugged him again. "Oh, Finley. I'm so proud of you."

"To be fair, Mr. Welsh paid me double what I asked. So I did the same amount of work for the money I earned today."

She laughed again. "Regardless, you saw a need and took the initiative to help someone who's practically a stranger. That is something to be very proud of."

Leah and Finn's List for an Awesome Summer

1. ~~Eat a whole gallon of ice cream (each)~~
2. ~~Build a throne~~
3. Take a dance class
4. ~~Hunt crabs at night, at the beach~~
5. ~~Sneak into an R rated movie at the theater~~
6. Drive a car
7. ~~Discover a new world~~
8. ~~Stay awake for 24 hours straight~~
9. ~~Find buried treasure~~
10. ~~Attempt a world record~~

24

"How was work?" Leah asked as Finn pulled up to her house just after 10 o'clock.

"It was good. I didn't have any troubles and got paid right away."

He intentionally left out the part about mowing Mrs. Jody's yard. It felt more meaningful to keep it a secret between him and his mother.

"Cool. Do you have everything you want to bring with? I have a notebook, a couple pencils and crayons with today—and lunch, of course."

"Yeah, I'm ready to go."

They made their way back to the new world, enjoying the sunshine and light breeze. It made their journey seem more charming, as though nature delighted in their discovery and was encouraging them to return over and over. When they reached the woods, they had an easy time retracing their steps because of the chalk markings Leah had left on the tree trunks. They turned left after reaching the end of her markings and quickly found the creek.

Two robins having brunch shrieked in surprise as Leah and Finn entered the little clearing. They chirped angrily in the trees, complaining about the disruption, before moving to a different area of the woods.

Finley stretched lazily and settled down on the ground, resting his back against a tree. Leah moved closer to the creek and laid on her tummy as she drew the scene in front of her—mushrooms, where ants sought shelter from the rain, flowers, which curtsied to each other when it was windy and water, streaming gently down the creek, as though it had all the time in the world and nowhere in particular to go.

"Finley," she said idly, "what are you going to do today?"

He opened his eyes and yawned. "Hmm?"

She chuckled. "You're not going to nap all day, are you?"

"No."

"Do you want to draw something? I have extra paper and pencils."

He thought for a moment. "Nah, that's OK."

"I wrote a story last night… Do you want to read it?"

"You wrote a story?"

She shyly nodded, suddenly feeling a little vulnerable about sharing her work. "Yeah, um…I've been writing since I got back from the cabin.

Something about nature inspires me and I've been enjoying it a lot."

"Really? That's wicked cool. Yeah, of course I'll read it."

She smiled and flipped through her notebook to the right page. "Only read this one. I'm still working on the other stories."

"I won't even peek at them." He grasped the book and settled back underneath a tree.

"Can you read it aloud?" she asked. "I wanna hear how it sounds coming out of someone else's mouth."

He smiled, excited at the opportunity to try out new character voices. "You betcha." He cleared his throat then began reading with a dramatic narrator voice:

In a faraway land across the sea, there was a little country and in this country was a forest so huge, no human had ever reached its center. Therefore, no human had ever met the magical beings that lived there. One of them was a troll. An old troll, with a crooked back, a nose too large for his face and skin the color of canned peas." Leah giggled quietly as he continued. "He lived in a tree with a hole in it and he'd complain to everyone around about his terrible life." Finley changed his voice with every character as he'd done with the ghost story earlier in the summer.

"This tree isn't big enough," the troll complained, in his scratchy voice. "Every night I cram myself in there and every morning I wake up with a stiff neck."

"I'm sorry, Mr. Troll," said the wise owl, who lived next door, "but I have four babies and even our tree, which is bigger than yours, is a tight fit for all of us. We can't switch homes."

Mr. Troll threw up his hands. "Bah. I don't want your crummy tree anyway. It's probably got termites."

"No, it's a very lovely home," the wise owl argued but Mr. Troll had already walked away.

He saw a couple crickets chattering to each other. They were discussing the newest songs their friend played last night at Club Cricket.

"You crickets," Mr. Troll sneered. "You play your music way too loud. And you can never whisper when you talk. It's always chirp this and chirp that. Don't you understand the value of quiet?"

The crickets looked at each other. "We're sorry to have bothered you," one said, shyly.

Mr. Troll continued, "You were so loud, you kept me awake all last night."

"We don't know how to chirp quietly," the shy cricket explained.

The other one said, "Perhaps, you should move somewhere quieter?"

"Bah. You crickets are everywhere. If I moved away, I'd just run across another Club Cricket."

Mr. Troll angrily stomped away. He was planning to make a mushroom stew for dinner so he went to Fungus Lane to look at their selection.

"All the mushrooms this year are bitter," he announced to anyone nearby, who would listen.

"Oh, I don't think so." A fairy twinkled as she fluttered by his ear. "I think they're very sweet. Have you tried the little red ones?"

"I don't need red mushrooms, I need the large, brown ones," he said indignantly. "You can't make mushroom stew with the red ones. They get too soft and lose all their flavor."

"I'm sorry, I don't think they have what you're looking for," the fairy explained.

"Bah," said Mr. Troll. "They never have what I need. I'll do my mushroom picking somewhere else."

Leah cut in, "What do you think so far?"

"It's good."

She pointed to a nearby tree. "Those are the red mushrooms in the story and the brown ones are here by the creek."

"Oh, yeah, that's cool."

"Sorry for talking, I'm just so nervous. It's weird hearing you read my story. Everything sounds so cheesy."

He started to close the notebook. "Do you want me to stop?"

"No…no, it's OK. You can keep going. I won't interrupt again."

Mr. Troll stomped away, muttering angry comments as he went. He looked all around but couldn't see the mushrooms he wanted. Finally, he found them but they were on the other side of the creek. There was no bridge to cross over but that didn't stop Mr. Troll. He was determined to get the mushrooms he wanted. It had been a dry year so the water was low. Mr. Troll climbed down a little of the way then jumped across the water and climbed back up on the other side.

He laughed in triumph. "Now I'll get what I want."

The troll shoved his pockets full of large, brown mushrooms and ate some along the way. There were so many mushrooms, he couldn't carry them all. He vowed to come back the next day with a bag.

Suddenly, the sky became black with thunderstorm clouds. A flash of lightning, a roll of thunder and bang; it started to rain. It sounded just as if thousands of maracas were playing at once. Mr. Troll found a bush to hide under until the storm stopped but he didn't realize the creek was filling up with water. When he finally came to his senses, it was too late. He couldn't make it across. He found an old log and pushed it into the creek, hoping to run across it. But the water was running too fast and it started to carry the log away. He held onto it, hoping to still make his plan work but the log scratched his knee and the current was so strong that he had to let go. He fell to the ground and looked at his knee. It was badly hurt. Running or jumping across was impossible. He was cold, miserable and had run out of options to get back home. A dark fog was settling on the land and it was getting close to nightfall. He didn't know what else to do.

In desperation he called out, "Help. Help, I'm stuck."

The wise owl, who had sensitive ears, heard him. She turned to her husband and asked, "Is that Mr. Troll?"

He listened along. "Yes, I believe it is. He's saying he's stuck. Well, where is he?" They scanned the area.

"There he is," said the wise owl. "He's lying on the ground, on the other side of the creek. I think he's hurt."

"There's a fog coming in," cautioned her husband. "If we don't get him soon, we won't be able to see anything as we're flying."

"We can help," offered the two crickets.

"Thank you," said the wise owl. "My husband and I will fly over. If we each grab him by the shoulders, I think we can fly back with him."

So, the two owls flew to Mr. Troll before the fog got too thick. They easily found him because of his screaming.

"Hush," instructed the wise owl. "You can stop yelling, we're going to take you home."

Mr. Troll stopped immediately and wiped his face. He didn't want them to notice he'd been crying.

He asked, "But how are we going to get back?"

The owls each grabbed onto his coat with their talons and flew up. The fog was so thick; they couldn't see anything in front of them. Thankfully, the two crickets on the other side of the creek chirped as loudly as they could so the owls could hear which direction to fly. When they reached the other side, they released Mr. Troll carefully on the ground and everyone gathered around.

"Your knee looks terrible," the shy cricket remarked.

"It hurts." Mr. Troll sniffled.

"I believe I can assist you." The fairy flitted to them, carrying a red mushroom. "I will quickly make a cream from this mushroom, which will heal your knee and make it feel better."

Mr. Troll was embarrassed and touched that everyone would help him, especially after he'd treated them badly.

"Thank you," he said, after he was bandaged and feeling much better. "I don't deserve to have you as neighbors and...you're not too bad."

Everyone smiled at him. They knew 'you're not too bad' was his way of saying 'I appreciate you'.

"Aww." Finley smiled.
"Did you like it?" Leah asked.
"Yeah. It was a really nice, gentle story. It's a great one for kids."
"What? Do you mean toddlers or older kids?"
"I dunno…toddlers?"
Leah frowned. "I don't want it to be for little kids. That's too cutesy. I want older kids to enjoy it. It's a modern fairy tale."
"If you want modern, maybe you should add a skateboard."
"Finn…"
His mind reeled with new ideas. "All right, how's this for an ending…'As everyone sat together, the fog suddenly began to get even thicker and it smelled funny, as though something was rotten or burning. They realized it wasn't fog after all…it was smoke. Then a dragon appeared and burned everyone up'."

Leah laughed. "No way. I like my ending better."

Finley laughed along. "Suit yourself."

They spent the rest of the day laughing, drawing and making up stories. Time seemed to pass differently in their new world. It stretched longer than a normal day yet it also felt shorter. They vowed to never reveal its location to anyone.

The next day was rainy and Leah's chalk markings were washed from the trees. For a few days, they tried finding the creek again but never managed to find it. They decided it may be for the best anyway; the spot wouldn't become boring or lose its magical quality as they got older. Their world would remain enchanted in their memories for the rest of their lives.

25

"Aw, come on. Do we have to do it?" Finley asked, on the phone.

"Yes." Leah insisted, "We made a deal. You chose to add 'build a throne' to our list and I chose 'take a dance class'."

He sighed.

"I signed us up for Tuesday's class. We have to be there at 1 o'clock."

"Fine," he mumbled. "How long is it?"

"It's only two hours."

"Then I guess it's not too bad but Bryce can never find out I took a dance class. He'd mock me for the rest of our lives."

Leah rolled her eyes, even though he couldn't see her. "Whatever. Bring a water bottle and a pair of good shoes. Oh, and wear clothes you don't mind sweating in."

"I can hardly wait," he said, sarcastically.

They rode their bikes to the dance studio on Tuesday. They hadn't realized how far it was from their neighborhood so they made it through the doors just as the instructor was telling everyone to put their things down and join her in the center of the room.

"Good afternoon, my name is Mrs. Inch and I'll be your instructor today. Thank you for coming. Before we begin, I want to remind you today is a trial class. If you're interested in continuing lessons, you're welcome to sign up for a three-month course, starting this fall. In addition to this course, we also offer ballet, ballroom and tap dance. If you'd care to further discuss the options we have at this studio, including scheduling and fees, please find me after class."

Not a chance, Finley thought.

"OK, everyone," Mrs. Inch continued. "Let's begin with some stretching. It's important we warm up our muscles before the real fun begins."

As she led the class with different stretches, Finley looked around the room. Most of the other people were younger than Leah and him, although there was a good mix of boys and girls, which made him feel a little better but only a little.

Did she even say what type of dance we're doing? He thought. *I should have asked Leah before we started. What were the other classes the instructor listed? Ballet, ballroom and what? ...Well, at least I know we're not doing ballet today.*

"Let's start learning a couple steps," the instructor said enthusiastically and turned on her boombox. Hip-hop music filled the room, its loud beat reverberated off the walls.

Leah smirked at Finley. "Oh yeah, if you haven't figured it out by now, this is a hip-hop dance class."

Finley wanted to shake her by the shoulders. "Are you serious? You couldn't have told me sooner?"

She chuckled. "Yeah, but I liked watching you squirm."

Mrs. Inch turned to face the large mirror, covering the entire back wall. "All right, can everybody see me in the mirror? Make sure you can also see yourself then match your dance moves with mine."

She shouted out simple instructions as she demonstrated them. The class followed along as best they could.

"This is hip-hop?" Finley whispered to Leah. "It's so slow."

Mrs. Inch continued, "Now move your feet. Right then left. Right then left. One and two, three and four. This is called the Two-Step. Let's speed it up. One, two, three, four. One, two, three, four. Great job, let's keep going."

Leah was smirking as he murmured, "I take it back."

She laughed. *This is a blast. The instructor's so good about finding the beat of the song and moving along with it. She makes it look so easy.*

"OK, we got the feet down. Now let's focus on the arm movements. Up and hold then bring them down and hold. Keep it to the beat. Ready? And again. Up and hold then down and hold."

"This is so much better than I thought it would be," Leah whispered to Finn.

"Let's bring it all together. Ready? One and two, three and four. Left up, right hold, left down, right hold. Let's do it again."

Finley fumbled a little when they put it all together but by the third repeat he followed correctly.

"Now to the pace of the song. Ready and one, two, three, four. One, two, three, four. Very good." Mrs. Inch stopped dancing and applauded the class. "How are we feeling? Do we need a water break already?"

"No," the class said in unison.

"Then let's keep going. Next, we're going to do the Box-Step. Watch my feet."

They followed along with the feet then arms then together.

"Now we're going to put these two dance moves together," she announced. "We'll start with The Two-Step then transition into the Box-Step. Ready?"

The class affirmed they were ready to start and followed along. Several of them didn't transition very well but they found the beat and caught up in no time. Half an hour later, everyone was sweating.

"Very good, very good." Mrs. Inch applauded again. "Let's take a short water break and catch our breath then we'll work on the Patty Duke."

Leah took a sip of her water then asked Finley, "So? What do you think?"

He put down his water bottle and admitted, "To be honest, I didn't expect this. I thought we'd be taking a ballroom lesson or something but this is actually fun."

She laughed at his excitement. "Yeah, it kinda makes me want to sign up for classes."

"Why don't you?"

She shrugged. "Maybe I will. We'll see."

"Everybody feeling good?" Mrs. Inch asked. "Are we ready to start again?"

"Yes," everyone announced.

The class had a quick recap of the Two-Step then moved onto the Patty Duke-Step and Knee-Elbow Crosses. With an hour of the class remaining, they took another short break.

"How are you feeling?" Leah asked, as she sipped her water.

"OK." Finley took a big swig from his water bottle. "It's the same as gym class."

"I know what you mean. My heart is pumping harder."

"Now that I think of it, I wish we could do this in gym."

Leah beamed. "That would be great. I'm totally using these moves during our school dances."

"Oh yeah, I forgot that was the reason why you wanted to take this class in the first place."

"I also thought it would be fun but I didn't know we'd be the oldest ones here. It's a little awkward, isn't it?"

Finn wiped off a bead of sweat from his forehead. "It's not too bad once we're all dancing. Besides, this way no one from school will know we're here."

"True." Leah smiled, feeling better.

"Everyone ready?" the instructor asked.

The class confirmed they were.

Next, they learned the Running-Man and the Brooklyn. The latter required a little more practice than any of the other dance steps but everyone agreed it was worth the effort.

Mrs. Inch clapped her hands. "For our big finale, we're going to put all these moves together. It's fine if you don't get it at first. We'll go through it slowly then speed up. Just follow along as best you can and have fun."

Leah and Finn didn't do everything perfectly but they grew in confidence as they practised and could catch up quickly when they faltered. It was tiring but way more fun than either of them had expected. After the two hours were up, Leah picked up a pamphlet from Mrs. Inch, which explained everything she needed to know if she continued taking lessons.

"I think you should go for it," Finley said.

Leah drank the last of her water. "What about you?"

"I don't know…" He hesitated and saw a hint of disappointment in Leah's eyes. He continued, "Don't get me wrong, it was a blast but I don't know if I can do it on top of my homework and mowing lawns. I was thinking about joining theater club, also."

Leah nodded understandingly. "That's fair. You have other commitments already."

"But if you decide to take more classes after all…" He smirked. "You could teach me everything you learn."

Leah chuckled. "Deal. I don't know if I'll take them, though. Look at these prices. Dance class isn't cheap and with Dad out of a job—" She stopped and realized she'd said too much.

"What?" Finley stared with wide eyes. "Your dad doesn't have a job?"

She fidgeted. "Well, no."

"Was he fired?"

"No, not at all. His old job was making him miserable so he quit."

"When did he quit?"

"This past Friday was his last day."

"Leah, I'm sorry. I didn't know."

She shook her head. "No, it's OK. I didn't mention it before because Dad didn't want anyone to know until it was official but now; he's done working there so it doesn't need to be a secret anymore."

"What's he going to do now?"

"He had a job interview yesterday that seemed to go really well. He's waiting to hear back from them now."

"That's great. I hope he gets it."

Leah smiled. "We all do. It's just what he was looking for, too. He'd be working in the finance department of a non-profit organization. They help ex-convicts restart their lives; for example, getting a job, learning how to keep a budget, finding an apartment in a good neighborhood. He'd be paid a tiny bit less than what he was making at his old job, which definitely shows how undervalued he was there but it won't strain our household budget. Plus, his hours would be more flexible so vacation time is easier to take."

"It's practically his dream job."

"It's definitely an answer to our prayers," she agreed and looked down at the pamphlet in her hand. "I think if he gets the job, I'll ask my parents about taking dance classes."

Finn hesitated. "And if he doesn't?"

She shrugged. "Maybe next year I can take them. Anyway, they're not as important as my family. Whatever happens, happens."

"You sound so old and wise. I have just the thing to make you young again…a slushie."

She laughed. "Lead the way."

Leah and Finn's List for an Awesome Summer

1. ~~Eat a whole gallon of ice cream (each)~~
2. ~~Build a throne~~
3. ~~Take a dance class~~
4. ~~Hunt crabs at night, at the beach~~
5. ~~Sneak into an R rated movie at the theater~~
6. Drive a car
7. ~~Discover a new world~~
8. ~~Stay awake for 24 hours straight~~
9. ~~Find buried treasure~~
10. ~~Attempt a world record~~

26

"Sunday is our last day of summer break," Leah said to Finley on the phone. "We should celebrate we finished our list."

"No, we still have one thing left."

"Finn, I changed my mind. I don't think—"

"Wait a sec." Finley removed the phone from his ear. "What did you say, Dad?"

Mr. Davidson entered the kitchen. "I said I'm going to the grocery store to pick up a couple things for your mom. I'll be back soon."

"Actually, that's perfect," Finley blurted then quickly tried to cover it up. "Uh, I mean…Dad, can I come with you?"

"You want to help me with the grocery shopping?"

Finley racked his brain for a reasonable answer. "No, I…was hoping we could stop by the new café on the way home."

"The one that opened last month? Why would you want to go there?"

"Uh, I don't want to go there but Leah does. I'm on the phone with her now." He held it up as proof.

"What are you saying? Did you say my name?" Leah asked.

He muffled the mouthpiece with his hand. "Leah said Diane's having a bad day or something…so Leah's hoping to cheer her up with a cup of coffee but it'll get cold if she bikes."

"All right. Let her know we'll pick her up right away." Mr. Davidson walked to the front door.

"Thanks, Dad." He brought the phone back to his ear and whispered, "Did you hear that?"

"No. What were you talking about?"

"Dad and I are coming over right now. Oh, and get your wallet. You're our alibi."

He hung up before she could say anything else then followed his father out the door. They were at Leah's house in mere seconds.

"Hi, Mr. Davidson." She smiled as she got into the backseat and gave Finley a dirty look.

"Hi, Leah. We're going to stop at the grocery store first then you can pick up your coffee on the way home. Sound good?"

"…Yep. Thanks." She looked at Finley and mouthed, "What are we doing?"

"Just wait," he whispered. "I'll explain later."

"It's very nice of you wanting to cheer up your sister," Mr. Davidson said, as he turned the car onto a smaller street.

Leah frowned at Finn, unsure how to answer.

"Yeah, she's a good sister," Finley said to break the silence.

"How has your summer been? I haven't seen you in a while."

"It's been good," she said, relieved she finally knew what to say. "My family went to my aunt and uncle's cabin for two weeks and I've just been hanging around since we returned."

"Good, good. Do you feel ready to start school on Monday?"

"Almost," she nodded. "Tomorrow, Mom's taking Diane and me shopping to get some new clothes and supplies for the school year."

Mr. Davidson turned into the grocery store parking lot. It was surprisingly empty for a Friday evening but he still parked in the middle of the lot.

"Here we go," he said, turning off the vehicle.

"Why did you park so far from the entrance?" Leah asked.

"I like to keep those spots available for the elderly," he explained, "so they don't have to walk as far."

"Oh, that's thoughtful." She unbuckled her seat belt.

"You kids can stay here, if you like. I don't expect to take too long."

Finley unbuckled, too. "Sounds good. Thanks, Dad."

Mr. Davidson grabbed a grocery cart before entering the store. As soon as he was out of sight, Leah demanded answers.

"OK, what is this all about?"

"Don't you see?" Finley asked. "This is our golden opportunity. We're gonna drive the car in the parking lot."

"Are you crazy?" Leah's eyes were huge. "We can't drive the car. That's what I was trying to tell you on the phone. It's illegal for us to do it."

"Come on," Finley whined. "We can get away with it. The parking lot is so empty, no one will know."

"I can't believe you're saying this. You want to break the law just because you think you can get away with it?"

He paused to consider the question. *Sure, I've become more mature this summer. I help out around the house and mow a couple lawns around the neighborhood. And when I think about it, I'm taking Dad's advice. To drive a car, I've made a plan, thought it out and now I'll complete it. This is the last item on our list and I'm going to follow through on this goal, especially if I can do it without getting in trouble.*

Of course, he knew this was a thinly veiled excuse to be rebellious and irresponsible but, at that moment, he didn't care.

"Are you going to drive?" he asked.

"No way," Leah insisted, "and you shouldn't either. What if you scratch the car?"

"I'll say a shopping cart hit it. Besides, I could just drive around the block. That's not too far. I know how to drive. I've just never done it before."

"No. No. No. You're not seriously considering this."

He paused again. *Should I do it? No. Will I do it? ...Yes.*

He leapt up and crawled into the driver's seat.

"Finn, don't do it." Leah pulled at his arm.

He ignored her and focused on the instrument panel.

"Finn, what if you hit someone else's car?"

He adjusted the seat so his feet could touch the pedals then he looked down and pressed the brake.

"Finn, we'll just do it a different year. It's the same as when we were going to change our new world task into a road trip. I mean, before we suddenly found the creek—"

He turned the key in the ignition and the engine rumbled to life.

Leah yelped. "Finn, stop. You're going to get into so much trouble. I don't want to be in an accident."

He put his hand on the gearshift and moved it to 'D'. Suddenly, he was nervous. *Wait. Everything Leah's saying makes sense. I'm crazy for even considering this. If anyone sees me, I'll be grounded for life. I might even get a criminal record...but I can't stop now. Leah would say I chickened out. She'd hold it against me forever, saying she's the smart, reasonable one while I'm an idiot who almost crashed Dad's car. I can't let that happen. I have to do something and I have to do it now.*

"Here we go." He held his breath.

Slowly, he removed his foot from the brake and applied it to the accelerator. The engine revved slightly and inched forward. Leah screamed but he barely registered it. His mind was racing. *At this rate, my grandma could walk faster than us. Someone will definitely see the car and wonder why it's moving so slowly.*

His palms were sweaty but he didn't dare remove them from the wheel to wipe them off. Little by little, he drove the car into the empty parking space in front of them. He quickly moved his foot back to the brake pedal and jerked the car to a stop, causing Leah to fly into the back of the seat ahead of her. She stopped screaming. Finley put the car in park, turned off the engine then slunk back into the backseat and buckled up. Leah stared at him and, for a moment, he was worried she was going to cry.

"I…can't believe…you did that," she hissed.

He cleared his throat and tried to sound older than he felt. "Well…now we can cross that off our list."

Leah rested her head on the backseat and stared at the car roof. Her voice was low and sounded forcibly calm. "If we were seen, I better not get in trouble for this."

Finley raised his chin defiantly. "I'll take all the blame and say you had nothing to do with it."

Leah looked at him and a sharp laugh burst from her throat. She tried to stop but couldn't manage to hold back her emotions. Finley was so surprised he began to laugh, too. They laughed harder and harder until tears formed in their eyes.

"I can't believe you drove a car," she exclaimed. "I mean, that was such a stupid thing to do but—but also so cool."

"We can't tell anyone," Finley said, between gasps of air.

"Never." Leah shook her head.

Finley caught a movement from the corner of his eye. "Oh, be quiet. It's my dad."

They were so scared, they immediately stopped laughing. They sniffled and wiped their eyes before he reached the car and loaded his bags of food into the trunk.

"I think we got away with it," Finley whispered, as his dad closed the trunk and walked to the car door.

"I don't think he noticed the car moved," Leah agreed.

"Hey, thanks for waiting," Mr. Davidson said, as he got in the car. He stopped for a moment and regarded the seat.

Panic showed on Finley's face as he and Leah made eye contact. He wondered, *Did I forget to move the seat back to its original spot?*

His dad readjusted the seat and muttered, "Huh, that's better."

Leah gave Finley an icy look. He gave a nervous shrug, in return.

Mr. Davidson glanced at them through the rear-view mirror. "OK kids, let's go. Leah, you wanted to stop by the new café that's about a block from here, right?"

She kept her eyes on Finley, unsure how to respond. After he nodded, she replied, "Uh, yeah. Thanks, Mr. Davidson."

"All right," he said. "Then let's get the show on the road."

He drove to their next destination and seemed completely unaware about the parking lot incident. Finley went in the café with Leah so he could explain why they were there in the first place.

After they dropped Leah at her home, he helped his dad put away the groceries. Meanwhile, Leah surprised her sister with the coffee (who wasn't having a bad day but still enjoyed the kind gesture). Leah and Finley didn't say a word about their rebellious event for the rest of the day. This was partially because they were worried they'd break out into hysterical laughter again and partially because of their guilty consciences. Naturally, Finley felt worse about it. One minute, he reveled in excitement but the next, he felt ashamed for betraying his father's trust.

Dad's been so proud of me lately. What would he think if he found out what I've done?

Meanwhile, Leah kept replaying the moment in her head, wondering if she could have done anything else to stop Finn and wondering, too, how it would feel to drive for the first time.

Leah and Finn's List for an Awesome Summer

1. Eat a whole gallon of ice cream (each)
2. Build a throne
3. Take a dance class
4. Hunt crabs at night, at the beach
5. Sneak into an R rated movie at the theater
6. Drive a car
7. Discover a new world
8. Stay awake for 24 hours straight
9. Find buried treasure
10. Attempt a world record

27

The oak tree leaves rustled and hung silhouetted against the starry sky. The nights were starting to get cooler and the crickets seemed to chirp louder. Finley climbed into the tree house, followed by Leah. This time they didn't have to meet in secret. They didn't need to cross off anything from their summer list. They settled among the pillows and blankets, each with a mug of warm cocoa in hand.

"I have something for you," Leah said as she reached into her pants pocket then dropped a shell necklace into Finley's hand.

"Thanks." He smiled. "Whoa, this is cool. Where'd you get it?"

"I made it from the shells we found at the beach. The day we found buried treasure."

"Are you serious? Wow, thanks, Leah."

"I tried making it at the cabin but didn't have the right supplies at the time. I had to take out a book from the library to learn how to make the little holes the string goes through. It took longer than I expected but, at least, I got it done before school."

Finley proudly put it on. "Hey, it kinda matches the one you're wearing."

She touched the white, spiralled shell on her necklace. "They can remind us of the great summer we had and, if anyone asks, we can honestly say we found the shells at the beach. We'll be the only ones who know the whole story behind them."

"I wish I'd gottten you something." Finn's smile faded a little.

"You don't need to. It was your idea to make our summer list. I couldn't have asked for a better gift."

"It was an awesome summer." He beamed and looked down at the list in his hand. "What should we do with this?"

Leah shrugged. "What do others do with secret information?"

"Burn it?"

"No," Leah exclaimed. "We can't do that. Look at each thing we crossed off. They bring back great memories. If we burned it, we might forget everything we got to do."

Finley considered this then said, "What if we keep it as a time capsule?"

"You mean we should bury it then dig it up again after twenty years?" She paused, imagining them as thirty-four years old, reminiscing about this very summer. "I like your idea but let's not bury it in your yard. Let's keep it here—"

"In the tree house," Finley finished her sentence. "That's perfect."

"This is where it all started."

"Absolutely; and I know exactly where it'll fit."

He folded the paper and wedged it between a rafter and the roof, in the southeast corner of the tree house. It just barely fit.

"And let's not wait twenty years," he said as he sat back down. "Let's wait ten years instead."

Leah nodded happily. "Deal."

"I can't believe it's the last day of summer break."

"I know. It flew by so fast."

Finley said incredulously, "We're starting high school tomorrow."

She laughed. "I know."

He looked at her. "Are you nervous?"

She winced and admitted, "A little but only because everything's gonna be new. It'll take a while to figure out where everything is, how everything works and which teachers are the best."

"Yeah."

"Are you nervous?"

"No," he said instinctively but when he noticed Leah searching his face, he admitted the truth. "Well…yeah, a little. It's a bigger school so we'll hardly know anyone there."

"At least we'll probably have all the same classes," Leah said, "and we know everyone in our grade."

He chuckled. "Yeah, who to trust and who not to."

"Hey, I never told you about Dad." Leah bounced onto her knees. "He got the job."

"What? The one you were telling me about? The dream job?"

"Yeah. He starts tomorrow. He's so excited."

"Good for him. Wait, does that mean you're taking dance classes this fall?"

"I haven't asked yet," Leah confessed. "Dad found out about his job on Friday night and we've been too busy celebrating and getting ready for school for me to mention dance. I'll ask later this week, after our excitement dies down."

He sighed. "It's a new start for him and us."

"I'll drink to that." She raised her mug.

Finn raised his, as well. "Cheers. To new beginnings."

"And to an awesome summer."

"We did things we only dreamed of doing when we were younger."

"To making the impossible possible," she added and they clinked their mugs together.

Finley's eyes sparkled with inspiration. "Maybe we should start a list of things to do while we're in high school…" He grabbed his small notebook and a pencil from the floor.

Leah sipped her drink and said coyly, "Hmm… What should we do first?"

Leah and Finn's Calendar for an Awesome Summer

July

Sunday	Monday	Tuesday	Wednesday	Thursday	Friday	Saturday
26	27	28	29	30	1	2
	Ice Cream				Crab Hunting	
3	4	5	6	7	8	9
		World Record Preparation	World Record		Awake 24 hours	
10	11	12	13	14	15	16
			Buried Treasure			
17	18	19	20	21	22	23
	Throne	Throne Cancelled	Throne	Throne	Throne	
24	25	26	27	28	29	30
			R-rated Movie			
31	1	2	3	4	5	6

August

Sunday	Monday	Tuesday	Wednesday	Thursday	Friday	Saturday
31	1	2	3	4	5	6
	Cabin	Cabin	Cabin	Cabin	Cabin	Cabin
7	8	9	10	11	12	13
Cabin	Cabin	Cabin	Cabin	Cabin	Cabin	Cabin Throne
14	15	16	17	18	19	20
Throne	New World	New World	New World			
21	22	23	24	25	26	27
		Dance Class			Drive a Car	
28	29	30	31	1	2	3
Last Day of Summer						

About the Author

E. Reimer was raised in a small, prairie community in southern Canada. Imagination was a huge part of her childhood as she spent hours listening to stories and creating her own games and worlds with her siblings. This influenced her to later obtain a Bachelor of Arts degree with a major in English and a split minor in theater and drawing from Brandon University. While she continues to enjoy escaping to fictitious worlds, a part of her is always relieved to find herself safe at home when her eyes lift from the page.

Check out her work at:
http://ereimerportfolio.weebly.com/

9 781088 196366